REAL ALPHAS BITE

THE ALPHA-HOLE DUET

C.R. JANE

MILA YOUNG

Dedication

To all our amazing readers who have stuck by our sides on our wild journey.
While we wanted to say we're sorry for the cliffhanger, and we really tried to avoid one in this book...
#sorrynotsorry
We love you guys.

Join Our Readers' Group

Stay up to date with C.R. Jane by joining her Facebook readers' group, C.R.'s Fated Realm. Ask questions, get first looks at new books/series, and have fun with other book lovers!

Join C.R. Jane's Group

Join Mila Young's Wicked Readers Group to chat directly with Mila and other readers about her books, enter giveaways, and generally just have loads of fun!

Join Mila's Group

The Alpha-Hole Duet
From C.R. Jane and Mila Young

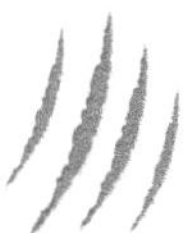

Real Alphas Bite
Book 1

I'm not in the habit of stealing women.

They come to me. They beg and plead for a taste of my power. My brothers and I rule the pack, crushing all challengers and scaring the rest into submission.

We're the nightmares that wake you up screaming, the devils you crave.

We have everything, so we want for nothing.

Until she came along.

From the first moment I laid eyes on her, I knew she was mine....ours.

We took her swiftly in the middle of the night, stealing her out from under her fated mate's clutches.

She was only meant to be a play thing, a passing fancy.

So why do I find myself watching her as she sleeps, protecting her... falling for her?

Real Alphas Bite can be read on its own. You do not need

to read any of the other stories in the Reject Island collection to enjoy this book. However, Real Alphas Bite will continue in Real Alphas Mate.

Syn

"**S**leep tight, little one," my daddy said as he tucked me in and gave me my favorite bear, Mr. Stuffins.

I yawned and pulled the blanket up to my chin, all the while studying the man leaning over me with a strange look in his eye. He'd been acting weird for months, full of energy one day and then unable to get out of bed the next. Mommy said he was just "going through grownup stuff," but I just wanted my daddy back. The man still staring at me was a stranger, and he gave me a weird feeling.

"No matter what, I want you to stay in bed tonight, do you understand, little one?" he asked as he abruptly grabbed Mr. Stuffins out of my arms and stared at him in fascination.

"Please give him back, Daddy," I begged as I reached out my arms for the bear I'd come to depend on lately. Daddy wasn't the only one who'd been acting strange; Mommy had been acting weird too, crying in her bedroom at all hours and screaming at Daddy for stuff I didn't understand.

Daddy tossed the bear at me and leaned closer until I was

shrinking back against my pillow, gripping Mr. Stuffins tightly against me. Daddy's teeth elongated into sharp points, and his eyes took on a yellow glow as a low growl pulled from his throat.

"Stay in your bed," he pressed, the rumble of his wolf pulsing through his voice with authority.

I nodded quickly, not wanting to make him any madder.

His teeth receded after he stared at me for another minute, and he must have believed me because he abruptly turned and left the room, shutting the door behind him. A moment later, I heard the click on my doorknob that let me know he had locked it. I didn't worry too much about that; my older brother Jamie had shown me how to unlock it using a pin, so if I had to use the restroom, I'd be able to get out.

I snuggled into my pillow, trying to ignore the flicker of unease in my stomach at the way my dad had been acting. Mommy had promised things would get better soon. She'd told me that Daddy had a plan, whatever that meant.

I just had to trust them.

)))

I woke up coughing and struggled to sit up. The room was hazy, and my eyes watered just looking around. Smoke. My room was filled with smoke.

I tried to yell for Mommy, but I immediately started coughing as soon as I opened my mouth and took in a huge gulp of smoke.

Grabbing Mr. Stuffins, I jumped out of bed and crawled along the floor towards the door. Tears rolled down my cheeks as I struggled to keep my eyes open so I could see where I was going. All I could taste was ash, and my breath was coming out in gasps. The smoke was streaming in from under my door, but it was the only way out; my room was on the second floor, and I'd never been able to successfully open my window without help from Mommy and Daddy. It was too old and heavy.

I grabbed the doorknob and let out a sob when I remembered that Daddy locked it. It was cool to the touch, though. That's a good thing, I think. They talked about fire safety at school, and I remembered Ms. Windrow had said something like that.

I coughed again and almost threw up. My throat was burning as I struggled to find the pin that Jamie and I had hidden between the baseboard and the carpet.

I gasped in relief when I found it and immediately started fiddling with the doorknob. For some reason, Jamie had made me practice for hours when Mommy and Daddy weren't around, making it into a game where he pretended we were bank robbers. So even with the smoke, I got the door to unlock in just a minute.

As soon as I opened the door, smoke began to billow inside my room. "Mommy! Daddy! Jamie!" I screamed before erupting in another coughing fit. No one appeared in the hallway, and I couldn't hear anything besides the sound of flames crackling and wood creaking and breaking from somewhere out of view.

I crawled down the hallway, stopping at Jamie's room. His door was cracked open, and I hurried and pushed it all the way forward.

A scream burst out of me when I saw Jamie lying on the ground right by the door with his arm outstretched like he'd been on his way out when he collapsed. I crawled frantically towards him and began to pull on his arm. At sixteen, he'd already shifted for the first time, and he was huge compared to me. But I wasn't about to leave him. He was my best friend. I tried to shake him, but he didn't respond at all. I put my head on his back, crying in relief when my head rose with one of his breaths.

Crying and coughing, I pulled on his arm, only able to drag him a couple of inches before having to take a break.

The smoke grew worse and worse as I continued to pull on my brother. I somehow drew us both into the hallway before being unable to get him any further.

"Please get up, Jamie," I cried, my hands shaking as I grabbed his arm again and shook him.

A low moan came out of him, and his eyes flickered open. Relief coursed through me as I patted his hair and tried unsuccessfully to get words out to tell him what was happening. He stared at me wide-eyed for a moment before beginning to cough. The coughing seemed to wake him up and get him to realize the situation though, because he abruptly shot up, almost knocking me over as he did so.

"Syn!" he cried in a raspy voice before grabbing my hand and starting to drag me down the hallway.

The smoke grew thicker as we made it to the hallway. We'd just turned into the kitchen when I screamed and pulled away from my brother, sprinting over to my mother who was lying on the floor in front of the oven. For a second, I thought she'd just passed out like my brother, but then I stepped into something wet and warm as I got closer to her, and even through the haze of smoke, I could tell it was blood.

My eight-year-old mind was struggling to comprehend what I was seeing.

"Syn!" my brother cried out as he reached me, going perfectly still when he realized our mother was dead. I fell to the ground and buried my face against her, my little body wracked with sobs as I pulled at her prone form, distraught.

Suddenly, a fiery beam fell to the ground in the living room, shattering the coffee table and sending sparks, fumes, and flames everywhere.

"Come on," Jamie cried as he tried to pull me from my mother.

"No," I cried out, struggling to hold on to her. Jamie wrestled me away and started to push me towards the front door, just down the hall from the kitchen. We had just made it to the hallway when Jamie cursed and stumbled back, pulling me protectively behind him.

"Why are you out of your room?" I heard my father roar.

I peeked my head out from behind Jamie and shrieked when I saw my father shift, his grey wolf massive and ferocious in front of us.

A second later, Jamie had shifted, and the two of them crashed together, the impact so great that the frames that hadn't fallen when the beam had dropped, all shattered to the ground.

I stood there frozen as my brother and father fought fiercely, neither of them holding anything back. My father outweighed my brother by at least a hundred pounds. My brother had just shifted for the first time; he was a long way off from matching my father in size.

"Please stop," I screamed, falling to my knees and crossing my arms around my body. I watched in horror as my father took a huge bite out of Jamie's shoulder. My brother's wolf howled in agony, and I stared in disbelief as my father lunged at Jamie's jugular for a killing strike.

Jamie barely missed having his throat torn out as he threw himself back. Jamie's wolf was whining in pain as he angled his body in front of me, trying to make sure my father couldn't get to me. Blood was seeping from his wound, and his whole body was shaking as he prepared for my father's next attack.

I could see the craziness in my father's gaze as he pushed back on his haunches, preparing to leap at us and end us both.

He flew through the air towards us just as another wooden beam—my mother had insisted on installing them along the ceilings—fell right on top of him. A sharp howl rushed out of him as my father crashed to the floor, pinned under the beam. But even with it on top of him, he was trying to struggle towards us wildly, his teeth bared and growls erupting from his throat.

My brother whined and collapsed in front of me before shifting back. Blood was still gushing from his shoulder, and I didn't understand why he wasn't healing. He was supposed to be healing.

"Jamie," I whimpered, putting my hands on his neck as if I could stop the bleeding.

Jamie took a deep breath before stumbling to his knees, trying to pull me away from my father and the beam that was now blocking the hallway.

We'd just made it out to the living room when another beam fell. The fire was coming from the hallway and from the living room, and we were trapped in the kitchen. There were flames everywhere, and at this point, I was gasping for breath, my head feeling light and fuzzy from the smoke.

Jamie stumbled to his feet and tried to lift a chair, only to drop it with a crash and a yelp of pain from pulling on his wounded shoulder.

In a daze, I stumbled forward to help him lift the chair, realizing he was going to try and shatter the kitchen window.

But as I walked, I tripped, the smoke finally too much for me to handle. I slumped over the table.

I faintly heard Jamie yelling at me, and then my eyes closed as I drifted into unconsciousness.

The crash of more beams falling roared around me. The sound of a wolf's growl pierced the air, and a mournful cry from my brother filled my ears.

The last thing I felt was the lick of heat burning at my skin.

Chapter 1

Syn

His laughter sliced through my skin.

Or at least that's what it felt like as Brayden's laugh echoed through the room. I didn't have to lift my head to make sure it was him. Everything about him was embedded in my skin, an unfortunate byproduct of the fact that Brayden Whitlock happened to be my fated mate.

My fated mate who had unequivocally destroyed my existence by rejecting me.

The reasonable part of my brain recognized his weaknesses. He was spoiled and proud. He lacked a conscience or at least the part of a person that actually cared about anything but himself.

But when the Moon Goddess chooses your fated mate, she also gives you this terrible wanting inside of you, this desire for the other half of your soul.

Even if the other half of your soul would be disgusting in any other circumstance.

Pain flickered in my gut as a female's voice intertangled with his. Just like I didn't have to look up to know his laugh, I also didn't have to look up to know that one of the beta-pack females was currently wrapped around him, trying to worm her way into his bed.

I couldn't think about that without nausea building.

How was it possible that I could still feel like this after everything, and he could go about his life like I had never existed.

Why did Brayden pretending like I never existed mean going out of his way to torture me?

Even knowing that I shouldn't, I glanced up, meeting Brayden's gaze, which immediately turned triumphant when he saw I was looking. He grabbed Desmonda's hair tightly and pulled, eliciting a squeal from her that I know made him hard. I'd learned the hard way that Brayden got off on pain.

The girls he hurt didn't seem to care though. The power that he held as the Alpha's son and future pack leader had them coming back for more again and again. Broken flowers that thought his power was like the sun and they had to gravitate towards him in order to grow.

"Get a new keg from the back," Devon, the other bartender on duty, barked at me. In a regular world, we would have been equals. He could have gotten his own fucking keg. But in the Madfur Pack, where I was considered the lowest of the low and basically a whipping girl to everyone above me, Devon could talk and order me to do whatever he wanted.

And he did.

I was Cinderella. But instead of three people trying to ruin my life, I had a whole pack. And no fairy godmother.

I headed to the back, already grimacing about my task. I was strong enough thanks to my wolf; that wasn't the problem. But the scarring all down my back and my butt, the pink, raised skin that never healed, made a lot of tasks difficult and painful.

Not that anyone around me cared.

"Grab the empty one," Devon snapped at my back.

My wolf growled inside of me, not happy, as usual, about being bossed around by someone she considered inferior, but she couldn't do anything about it. I glanced down at the thin bronze band that encircled my wrist, ensuring that my wolf couldn't show herself.

I'd been allowed to shift once, only so I didn't "go mad" like wolves in the old pack legends. And after that brief, glorious moment of meeting her, the most beautiful creature I'd ever come across, the bracelet had been snapped on and had remained there ever since.

It was ironic that the person with the power to free me was the person most likely not to.

I didn't bother answering Devon; he knew I wouldn't fail to obey. When you had scars on your skin like I did, whips and belts had quite the effect.

I took a deep breath and lifted the empty keg up, gritting my teeth as the exertion pulled on my fragile skin. Tears gathered in my eyes, and I choked out a cry.

I would have run, but I was trapped here, eyes on me every second to make sure the pack slave couldn't escape. Even now, a beta with glittering eyes leaned against the wall in the hallway, watching me struggle with a sadistic glint in his eyes.

My wolf clattered about inside of me, yapping at me to pick the damn thing up and not show any more weakness...or drop the keg on the beta.

I waddled down the hallway, because there was no graceful way to carry something that heavy, and made it into the back storage room where we kept the kegs and the rest of the alcohol. I'd just set the keg down when I heard familiar voices approaching from the direction of the Howler Bar offices.

"Did you see the notice? They're calling for all the rejected mates to be delivered to Reject Island for processing," Leon, the Alpha's top beta, whispered.

"Over my dead body," the Alpha growled. I froze, realizing

that they were talking about me. There weren't many of us. After all, who was terrible enough to be rejected when the mate bond was gifted by the Moon Goddess herself?

It was an exclusive club.

My wolf growled in frustration at my self-pitying monologue, and I took a deep breath, shaking off the familiar feeling of pain beginning to seep into my bloodstream.

For a second, I wondered what it would be like to get away from here. Everyone there would be just like me, a cast-off that the world didn't want. I could have a new life. Have friends... maybe even love. I almost laughed at that last thought.

Except there had to be a reason for sending rejects there, right? They were afraid of what we would become without the mate bond. The alleged special little curse only affected the ones who were rejected, not the ones who did the rejecting. Wasn't that a nice little side effect?

"They're sending officials to all the packs to ensure the decree is followed," Leon warned.

The Alpha snorted. "Like our pathetic little bird would squeal if they came. She knows better than to bite the hand that feeds her."

My wolf bristled at being called "pathetic" and "a bird", but I'd been called that so many times it was almost the same as calling me a redhead.

"Wouldn't it be easier just to be done with her?" Leon asked, tentatively. I stood up straighter, straining my ears not to miss a single word. I'd never understood why I was still kept here. You would have thought they'd want me as far from their perfect Brayden as possible. Even though the pack glorified him, I was the blight on his reputation they couldn't forget. They couldn't help but wonder if there was something wrong with Brayden that he had been cursed...with me.

"We've had this conversation before, and I'm not keen on

repeating myself," Alpha growled, and a small whine escaped from Leon in the face of the Alpha's dominance.

I sighed, realizing I wasn't going to get any answers. And I wasn't going to waste a second worrying about Reject Island. The Alpha would find a way to make sure I never made it there, that was clear.

"I'll have the sentries keep an eye out for the officials so we will have warning," Leon answered subserviently, wisely realizing that the Alpha wasn't going to change his mind.

The Alpha snorted, like being worried about the government coming into town was the least of his worries. I listened as their footsteps faded away before going back to my task, pushing any thoughts of Reject Island out of my head.

I'd just bent over to pick up the new keg when I felt *him*.

Brayden.

Of course, it wasn't enough to torture me by having to see and hear him. He had to follow me back here too.

"Looking good, Syn," Brayden commented, obviously sizing up my ass from his vantage point just outside the door.

For a second, I was tempted to just ignore him, but I knew from experience that it would only make it worse. For a guy who had sent our relationship to the farthest reaches of hell... he just couldn't completely let me go.

"Thanks, Bray," I said, wincing as the nickname slid off my tongue...probably similar to how Syn had slid off his.

I'd once been wildly in love with him and everything I thought he represented. He'd taken that devotion and used up every inch of it until I'd given him everything.

And as soon as he'd gotten that, he'd done what he'd always planned on doing; he cast me away.

I forced myself to meet his gaze, trying not to remember how it felt that day, trying not to remember how the word "reject" had sent fissures down my spine and how it had felt like I was missing something ever since that day.

And as much as I wanted to hate him, I couldn't blame him. Not really. Even if it was the Moon Goddess' wish, no one in this pack would have ever wanted to be with me. Not after what my father did.

Besides massacring at least five members of the pack, including Brayden's older sister, he'd set fire to our house after shooting my mother and drugging my brother. He'd meant for me to die in my room that night too, but of course, I'd woken up. Even after waking my brother up, my father had been sure to finish the job by tearing him to shreds while Jamie had tried to save me. I shivered when I thought about the moment I'd woken up in the hospital and realized that everyone I'd loved was gone.

The scars on my back and ass might be an outward reminder of my trauma, but I was certain the scars on my insides were much worse.

So no, I didn't blame Brayden for rejecting me. But I did blame him for making me fall in love with him, taking my virginity, and then casting me out in front of the entire pack.

That I did blame him for.

Brayden showed no sign that he was suffering from the same feelings I was. All I saw was lust in his eyes even though I knew firsthand he wasn't fond of what was underneath my clothes. Looking at my scars, you couldn't forget my father's sins.

I jerked my gaze away from him and heaved the full keg up, briefly squeezing my eyes shut from the pain. It felt like the skin on my back was about to tear. Of course, Brayden made no move to help me.

Awkwardly, I tried to move past him, but he put an arm out, blocking my way. I dropped the keg, unwilling to deal with the pain when I didn't know how long Brayden's bullshit was going to take.

"I've been thinking about us," he said with a grin I'd once thought was sexy.

"Was that before or after you fucked one of the betas?" I asked, noticing the red lipstick on his collar.

I clamped a hand over my mouth the second it came out, shocked I'd actually said that out loud.

Brayden looked shocked too before he got a grip on himself and let out a dark chuckle.

"The smart mouth is new, Syn," he said with a grin that showed off his pearly white teeth.

My stomach clenched. Once upon a time, I'd wanted him to know everything about me.

I pursed my lips and picked up the keg again, managing not to grimace this time, which was in itself a miracle.

I ducked under his arm, and he huffed out a laugh.

"I still think about that night, baby," he called to me as I made my way steadfastly down the hallway.

My hands shook around the keg as I struggled not to cry... or drop the keg and punch him in the face.

I did everything I could to not think about that night.

I trembled as I slid my shirt off my body, tingles cascading across my skin as I felt his gaze watching me hungrily. My breath came out in soft pants as he leaned against the wall, fisting himself as he stared.

Was I really going to do this? We were mates. The Moon Goddess herself had proclaimed it. He was the guy that everyone wanted, including me. I'd heard the rumors about the girls he'd been with, but this was different. He had to feel this same pull. This light inside of me that was solely focused on him.

Brayden slid his pants off and then ambled towards me as I stood there trembling, a mix of fear and desire coursing through my body. He wrapped an arm around me, freezing when he touched the warped skin...

He hadn't been able to hide the disgust he'd felt that night after seeing my scarring, but it hadn't stopped him from taking my innocence.

He pulled out of me and rolled to his back, huffing out a long breath before sliding out of bed all the way and throwing on his clothes. I pulled the covers up to my chin, watching him, confused.

"Where are you going?" I asked.

He grinned at me, the same grin that had girls throwing themselves at him for any crumb he was willing to give. This grin had one thing those others did not, though—a lick of cruelty that had my stomach shriveling up with dread.

"You didn't really think that the future Alpha of the pack would end up with the daughter of a murderer, did you? Especially the scarred daughter of a murderer?" He spat the words out like it should have been obvious to me this whole time. And, of course, it had seemed too good to be true, that someone like him would ever be interested in someone like me.

But the Moon Goddess...

He laughed scornfully, pulling my attention back to him. "Ahh, you did think that. Let's make it super clear so there's not a misunderstanding. Emersyn Landry, I reject you as my mate and cast you away from me forevermore."

Something shattered inside of me, and I hunched over, my breath coming out in gasps as the light inside of me that had been for him shriveled up and disappeared.

My steps hitched for a moment, but I kept walking down the hallway. Fated mate or not, Brayden was an asshole, and I would never make a mistake with him again.

"Don't take another step," he ordered, the Alpha power threading through his voice.

I froze, my wolf growling desperately inside of me. But there was nothing she could do...nothing that I could do either. I dropped the keg, the loud thump echoing through the hallway. I didn't bother to turn and look at him. I didn't owe him anything.

His footsteps sounded down the hallway until he was standing right behind me, his breath falling softly on my skin. I shivered, but not because it felt good.

"Kiss me," he ordered softly, the same power sounding from his voice. A teardrop trailed down my face, and I quickly wiped it away. I fought every move that my body made to turn around and obey him, but it was no use. My lips met his, and I shuddered with revulsion as his tongue dipped into my mouth. His arm reached around my waist to squeeze my butt, and a soft cry slipped from my mouth in fear of what he would do next.

He'd enjoyed torturing me since his rejection, enjoyed ordering me to serve him while he was on dates and with his friends, but he'd never forced me to do anything sexually.

My wolf whined inside of me. If I'd been allowed to shift, she would be trying to tear him to shreds right now, or at least tear off his manhood so he could never use it on anyone again.

He finally pulled his lips from mine, smiling smugly and staring down at me like he thought I'd be panting off of him. I made sure not to move. I didn't want to do anything to trigger his hunter instinct and push him to go further.

"Still sweet as sin," he murmured, a sadistic gleam in his eyes. I barely held in my scoff at his attempt at cleverness. Like he was the first one to say something like that, especially with the fact that I was indeed the daughter of a murderer. "Syn" and "sin" had gone hand in hand my entire life.

"I need to get back to work," I said in a surprisingly level voice considering I wanted to scream or cry. Or maybe both.

"Send over another bottle of my favorite, first thing," he ordered.

"Of course," I responded, making sure not to meet his eyes.

"Talk to you soon, Emersyn." The words were a promise, and it was all I could do to hold in another shiver.

What was I going to do if he went further? What could I do?

I'd kill myself before I let him take anything else from me.

He let go of me, and I cleared my throat before slowly picking up the keg again and walking down the hallway away from him. I could feel his gaze on me the entire time.

It was weird to actually feel relieved as I made my way back into the bar, even with Devon barking at me for taking so long and leaving him to actually work.

I hustled over to the bar and started filling drink orders. Out of the corner of my eye, I saw Brayden saunter over to his table from the back hallway, a beta girl immediately pouncing on him. He turned and shot me a wink before dipping her backward and making out with her messily. It was a good thing wolves couldn't spread most diseases. That kiss could have given me a million things considering how much his mouth and every other part of him got around.

A splash of cold liquid suddenly went down the front of my dress, and I gasped in shock as I focused from Brayden to the three girls standing there in front of me, all of them wearing identical evil smiles and looking like they all visited the same plastic surgeon and had asked for the same face.

"Whoops. Another, girl."

I gritted my teeth, and my wolf lurched up inside of me. I didn't even know these girls' names. I'd never been welcomed into any girl groups after what my father had done, and after a while, all of the women in the pack just blurred together. They all were the same. They all treated me like I was nothing.

A spilled drink down my clothes was nothing compared to what I'd been through in this pack.

My wolf whined again as I mechanically went through the

motions of pouring them another drink, my mind trying to think if there was any way out of here except for death.

But even as appealing as that was, it seemed like a slap in the face to my brother's sacrifice to ever do something like that.

I just didn't know how much more I could take.

Raucous laughter filled the air again, but this time, Brayden couldn't draw my gaze. I would get through this night just like I had all the others.

By keeping my head down and dreaming about the life I would have if I ever managed to escape this place.

Chapter 2

Hendrix

Murder was a noose I wore wherever I went.

Crossing the border into the Hallow Sector where the Madfur pack lived, I clenched and unclenched my hands as I prepared to teach the local Alpha a lesson on dishonoring our agreement. If everyone stayed in line and did their shit, we wouldn't have a problem.

I wasn't an unreasonable man, but no one disrespected me and lived to say a fucking word about it.

I entered through the heavy, metal door into Howler Bar, and the place fell silent upon my entrance; only the jukebox played a slow, depressing ballad. The door banged shut behind me, and a few of the wolf shifters flinched. Good. Let them be scared. The place brimmed with the scent of whiskey and the reeking musk of too many wolves crammed into the place.

Their leering eyes belonged to desperate pack members trying to carve a life in this pathetic, broken world.

When I glanced ahead to the bar, no one met my gaze, and a few vanished quietly out of the way, lowering their heads. There was no sign of Anton, the local Alpha, either, or his useless son.

I'd learned plenty in my twenty-eight years. The thing was, confidence intimidated people, as did silence. And I had no problem waiting for however long it took for them to show their faces.

I moved to a nearby empty table, and I took a seat with my view to the bar, watching when the bartender hurried over with a frothing glass of beer.

"Compliments of the house," he murmured, his voice shaky, and before I could ask him about Anton or his son, he rushed back, eager to leave my side.

I gulped down several mouthfuls of the cold beer, chasing away the heat from my throat.

Hushed whispers floated around me; the words *Khan's pack* and *Alpha Warlord* filtered through the room against the backdrop of the slow song.

Of course, they recognized me. I was the Alpha Warlord to the Khan pack, who ruled over this territory with my two brothers, so there was reason to fear me.

You didn't become the leader by being the good guy.

I was a self-proclaimed psychopath, and I wore the title as a badge of honor.

Every fucker in the place would love to stand up to me... but they didn't have the balls to kill as ruthlessly as me. If anyone bothered to try, I'd rip their fucking face off.

Because running a pack, and managing a lucrative arms trafficking business, while providing round-the-clock protection to the packs in our territories wasn't for the weak-hearted. My brother River once quoted a line he'd read somewhere: *Killing one man made you a murderer. But butchering thousands made you a king.*

Not that we'd disposed of that many...yet.

I wasn't visiting the bar to reminisce, though. In fact, I was beyond irate to be in this backwater town.

I scoured the bar again, roaming over faces when my sights

finally set on Brayden, the Alpha's son, emerging from a back area and crossing the room toward the bar. My wolf surged forward, knowing full well we were about to have some fun.

Brayden leaned an elbow against the bar, half propped up on a stool, with his two buddies laughing next to him. They had a young blonde near them, who seemed to be trying to pull away from their grip. Despite Brayden looking bored, he slid his fingers under her chin, lifting her head, studying her.

The fragile blonde froze on the spot. Unmated females were fair game and often used for rutting, then tossed aside. The world *was* fucked up.

Brayden acted every part the Alpha's son—arrogant and entitled. I had no issues with that. What he did wasn't my concern, unless it impacted me. And whether he knew it or not, his father's actions had placed him directly in my line of sight.

I lifted my drink to my lips to finish it when a sliver of red movement caught my attention over the rim. I slowly lowered the glass to the table and glanced over at her standing behind the bar.

Luminous green eyes as bright as a meadow. They immediately drew my gaze...they seemed to almost jump out from under long eyelashes as she wiped the bar counter furiously, anger burning across her face. She wasn't looking my way, but I was sure as fuck enjoying the show.

Something about her messed with my thoughts. I never had a problem with women. Most threw themselves at me, and they rolled over in submission, doing as they were told instantly.

But this little creature had me intrigued. Red hair so dark, it almost glinted purple beneath the lights. It cascaded around her face and fell down her low-cut neckline. The two white clips in her hair did little to tame the wild strands.

Her delicate jawline, high cheekbones, full lips, and

almond eyes made her beyond captivating. Why did someone like her work in this dead-end bar?

Tossing the rag somewhere behind the counter, she blew a long breath before marching out from behind the bar.

My gaze followed her as she stepped to the side of the room in her blue dress and black apron, her arms and legs dusty with dirt. Even in her loose clothes, I made out her tight, curvy body and an ass I'd love to see bright red with my handprint. The thought of her bent over had my cock stirring.

She lifted a wooden crate, clearly struggling with it, but no one aided her. Not even the two men nearby who appeared to work at the bar. She persisted regardless and wobbled out of the room with the box in her arms.

A sense of innocence came to mind when I looked at her, my wolf awakening in my chest as I studied her. Yet something about this beautiful girl reminded me of dark things... as though she was no stranger to the ugliness of this world.

She was an exquisite thing living in a tragic world. That was a travesty in itself.

I kept staring at the doorway in the back that she'd vanished through, the idea of going after her lingering at the forefront of my mind. The temptation to corrupt such an innocent-looking girl intrigued me, along with the notion of finding out what made her tick.

Once I broke her, she could never go back to how she was before.

I took a swig of my beer. There wasn't anything I could give the red-haired girl better than she had here...unless darkness was her kind of kink. My cock twitched once more in my pants, and I smirked. Both of us wanted to grab her and show her how to be fucked, but I didn't have time for that today. Not when I had to deal with this pack's disobedience in crossing me.

Going after her and grabbing her wasn't an idea I should entertain.

I steeled myself and climbed to my feet, turning back to Brayden. My boots thumped against the floorboards, announcing my approach toward the bar.

Brayden's friends spotted me first, and they scrambled out of there fast, but not Brayden. He was too busy with the little blonde he'd trapped.

I nudged the girl aside with a hand, and she stumbled over Brayden's feet and right into a nearby table. Only then did I notice the bruise under her eye, the puffy lip from where someone had hit her.

"Get out of here," I told her over my shoulder, my Alpha voice out in full force.

The bastard in front of me snarled, his head jerking up to me.

I caught him around the throat and picked him up, holding him in the air before he could even respond. It didn't take long for his face to go pasty white from fright.

My fingers constricted, and he wheezed, clawing at my arm, kicking the stool onto its side. A silent scream painted his mouth. Panic swirled behind his eyes, and I grinned at his alarm. I might not know this man well, but in this world, everyone was guilty of sin. I doubted anyone would miss him.

Deep in his stare, the darkness in his soul stirred, filled with the heinous things he was capable of. He gave off that vibe.

"Y-you got your eyes on that trashy, blonde bitch? She's yours." He gasped around my squeezing fist. "She always needs a good beating first, though."

I shoved him into a backbend over the counter. "That was just for fun. No, I'm here because your father is overdue with his payment, so you'll do."

I should have sent one of my men to deal with this, but as

my brother River reminded me, nothing gets the sheep to pay up like the big warlord himself paying a personal visit.

Fine by me to be made out as the villain.

Brayden choked, clawing at my hand, while I let my stare roam the room for his father. Still not here. What a shame... guess he'd find out later what crossing the Khan pack had cost him.

Brayden's idiotic friends were in my line of sight on either side of me. They'd seal their fate if they attacked me.

I leaned over Brayden. "Let's go outside and settle the payment, shall we? Unless you prefer I paint your father's bar in your blood?" Pulling back up, I wrenched him by his neck and hauled him to his feet.

I loosened my hold slightly, enough for him to hungrily gulp air. "Any last words? Want to ask for forgiveness for the shit I'm sure you've done?"

His eyes were frantic and huge, flicking to his friends for help, then back to me. "Fuck you! I've heard stories about you. You're a psychopath," he snarled.

"I like to think of it as being creative."

He threw a punch at my face. Brave idiot.

Swiftly, I snatched his fist with my free hand and bent his wrist backward, the snap of bone resonating. His face twisted as he howled, and behind me, the rapid footfalls told me patrons were running out of there. For good measure, I let go of Brayden and slammed my fist into his face hard. Fuckhead.

His friends winced, and I snarled in their direction, to which they made a speedy escape.

Blood spurted from Brayden's busted-up nose, but I had barely even started with him.

He tumbled to the floor, holding his bleeding nose. His eyes bulged as he glanced up at me.

I shook myself. "Looks like we're doing it in the bar then."

Kneeling down, I snatched a handful of his shirt and

hammered two more punches into his face, just in case he thought I was joking. He didn't seem like the sharpest tool in the shed.

"It's nothing personal to you," I stated as he slumped on his back, gurgling blood. I pulled out a blade from the sheath on my belt and slashed it across his face.

He cried out, rearing back and throwing his arms out to block me, but blood pebbled over his nose and cheeks.

Someone behind me shrieked.

I twisted to look around at an older woman watching us with horror on her face. Then she ran out of the bar with everyone else. Better this way. Decorating was hard when people got in the way.

Back to Brayden, he shook, wiping the blood with the back of his hand, the other hand lying twisted on his chest. "You're a fucking lunatic, man. I've done nothing to you."

"Now, I've been pondering a question the entire trip here. Do I skin you or slice you up? Do you have a preference?"

A terrified cry spilled past his lips as he became aware of the guillotine of my words hanging over him. With it, the putrid stink of piss hit my nostrils. A dark, wet stain spread across his brown pants from his groin.

"No happy endings for you, I'm afraid." I grabbed his neck, needing him to stay down.

"Don't kill me," he begged, attempting to drag himself backward and away from me.

"Hendrix," a panicked male's voice called from across the room, and I recognized him instantly.

Ah, about damn time the Alpha of Madfur showed up. Paybacks were more effective when the man who crossed my brothers and me was present.

I got up and pressed a boot down on Brayden's chest to keep him in place as I twisted my attention to Anton.

The white-haired man rushed over to me, grief-stricken at

the sight of his son beneath my heel. The fear on his face was palpable. He knew exactly why I was here. I remember the first time we entered the Howler Bar to offer him our protection, it took some convincing to get his agreement. I'd always known he was a wild card, and perhaps I'd been too lenient by letting it go this long before he paid us our quarterly dues.

"You ignored our reminders," I sneered, not giving him the chance to bore me with his bullshit lies. "Do you think my protection comes free of charge?"

He swallowed loudly, and I could smell his perspiration. "Hendrix, please, I have the money. I just needed a bit more time to gather it. I've got it locked up in the back, I can get it now. I've even put an additional ten percent for paying late."

"Am I supposed to be flattered?" I snarled. "You're still late and disrespected our agreement."

He shivered violently, his attention darting to his son on the floor. He lifted his calculating gaze my way, knowing he'd come to the end of the road. One way or another, someone was losing their life today.

He fell to his knees before me, grasping my shirt. "Not my son, please. Anything you want, it's yours, just not him." A whimper rolled over his throat.

I shoved his hand to brush him off me. "Get up," I growled. "I'll ask you only once. Someone has to pay. So, will it be you or your son?"

Anton stumbled to his feet, while Brayden squirmed beneath my boot.

The Alpha nervously licked his lips and kept staring at his son like he might start crying.

"I-I'm s-sorry..." Anton stuttered.

Footsteps drew my attention to the back door where the gorgeous red-haired beauty burst into the room, completely unaware of us. When she spotted us, she paused mid-step, staring at Anton. A quick scan of the empty bar made her cheeks turn ashen. She couldn't see Brayden or she would have reacted to him being all bloodied.

Instead, she stood there all doe-eyed. All vulnerable.

Our gazes clashed, and something shifted behind her eyes, her breathing coming quicker. She truly was a beautiful thing.

I noticed her lip trembling. She knew something wasn't right in the bar.

My chest tightened at her beauty, at the innocent look that masked something darker. For all I knew, she was concealing a knife under that dress to survive in such a town. By the look of things, she wasn't well cared for. She appeared beaten down, too fragile to harm. And that made me toy with the idea of finding out exactly how much darkness she lived with.

I'd fucked plenty of women, but none had called to me like her. None had my wolf growling in my chest.

"What do you want, Syn?" Anton barked. "Ain't you got work to do?"

Her cheeks blushed, and she hastily lowered her lashes. She spun on her heels and rushed out the back door.

Syn... I couldn't help but grin at the irony of her name.

When I looked at Anton, he watched me with a narrowing stare.

"We can make a deal," he stated with a nervous voice, then quickly licked his lips. "I see the way you stare at Syn. She's yours along with the payment, and we're even for last quarter's dues."

"Father," Brayden groaned, and I'd almost forgotten he was under my heel. Like I said, I doubted many would miss him if he died. "You can't!"

I had no idea what the girl meant to Brayden, but from his reaction, she must mean something, and that in itself sweetened the deal.

"You want to die, son?" Anton barked, then straightened his posture, looking me in the eyes. "What do you say? Deal?"

His breathing quickened. This man was a conniving opportunist.

Temptation pounded in my chest cavity, my thoughts drowning in images of such a pretty thing being mine. My brothers would be pissed, of course they would, but when did I care about their reaction?

I lifted my attention back to the rear doorway. She was a complication I hadn't anticipated.

"Deal?" Anton persisted, and his voice raked on my nerves.

"I'll think about it," I snapped. "Now, deliver your payment."

He flinched back, nodded, and made a hasty retreat through the back exit too.

An excited sensation curled in my gut at the notion of playing with Syn. At pushing her...

"She's not yours to take," Brayden groaned. "Emersyn is mine."

My wolf snapped, the sound grazing across my throat.

I lifted my boot and shoved my heel onto his broken hand, pressing down, to which he cried out.

"We'll see about that."

CHAPTER 3

SYN

I woke with a start, the sensation that something was wrong washing over me. I lived in a small loft over the bar that consisted of a tiny futon mattress, a single burner stove and sink, and then a bathroom with a small shower that only gave out cold water. It was a hovel, but it was *my* hovel. The only sanctuary I had in this pack.

And my wolf could tell something was wrong.

I sat up and blinked in the darkness.

It only took a second to see him. The place was too small for anyone to hide.

The stranger I'd seen for just a moment at the bar was leaning against the door, his overwhelming presence and scent sliding over me.

I fumbled for the steak knife I kept right by my futon, the only thing I had for protection without my wolf.

"It's not there, little wolf," he said, his gravelly voice washing over me. My wolf immediately quieted inside of me, so still I could almost picture her laying down and relaxing in the sun.

Traitor, I muttered inwardly.

And I swore my wolf just yawned.

"She likes me, doesn't she?" he murmured, like he could see inside of me right at that moment. I inched backward in bed, my gaze still darting around the tiny, dark room like a weapon was going to appear in front of me suddenly.

The stranger took a step forward, and I squeaked, "Don't take another step..." He chuckled darkly as if I was amusing him.

"I mean it. I'll scream. The whole pack will hear you. They'll all come." I tried to sound convincing. I actually wasn't positive that anyone in the pack would show up if I needed help. But he didn't know that.

He chuckled again, like I was this cute thing intentionally amusing him. "I might like it if you scream. But it won't do you any good. No one will come for you. You belong to me now."

My stomach clenched. I belonged to him? I ignored the warm sensations I felt at that comment. A therapist would probably have a field day with someone like me, a girl who'd had all affection withheld from her since she was little.

He took another step forward. Even in the darkness, there was a possessiveness in his gaze. A look that backed up his strong words. I eyed the window next to me, wondering just how badly I would get hurt if I tried to jump. If I could even do it fast enough for him not to stop me...which would never happen.

Two more steps and he was already right at the edge of my futon. His gaze was warm and hot as it trailed over my skin, and I realized belatedly that I'd let my sheet drop. I was sitting there in nothing but a spaghetti strap top and a tiny pair of shorts. And of course, because the things weren't comfortable enough, I was braless.

"You like the sound of that, don't you, little wolf," he purred the question as my own wolf purred back. She'd never acted like this before. It was almost a good thing I couldn't shift at this moment, because who knows what she would've done. She'd probably be humping his leg right now.

He shifted, and the moon streaming in from the window lit up his features.

He was... Beautiful. I'd known that from the little glance I'd had of him in the bar. But seeing him this close...There were almost no words. Beautiful was the only way to describe him. Dark messy locks, like he'd just gotten done running his fingers through his hair. His features were like the Moon Goddess herself had gathered up all the perfection in the world and decided to put it on his face. He had full pouty lips... And those eyes, I'd never seen eyes like that. In the moonlight, they looked like they were almost glowing. The light blue color reminded me of ice glittering under the moonlight.

Okay, Syn, get yourself together. I usually had more self-preservation than lusting after a mystery man who had broken into my room.

"You need to get dressed. I'd like to leave as soon as possible," he said, his gravelly voice rolling over me.

My wolf perked up even more. She liked the sound of that.

Me? I was both intrigued and terrified.

"I'm not going anywhere with you," I told him emphatically, crossing my hands over my chest when I felt my nipples begin to pebble under his hot gaze.

"I'm afraid that's not an option," he replied as he finally dragged his gaze away from me and took in our surroundings with a disdainful look. "Surely you must want more than this? More than a pack that would trade you away at the first chance?" he asked as he brought his attention back to me.

I stiffened at that news, although the sharp blade of betrayal I thought I would feel after hearing that never came.

I was nothing but a slave to this pack, a reminder of the dark blight in their history that they were forced to face every day. Honestly, it was a surprise that this hadn't happened before. Looking back at my Alpha's conversation that I'd overheard, it was surprising that they hadn't jumped at the chance to send me to Reject Island. I was a hard worker, and they all clearly enjoyed bossing me around, but I was still little more than a slave.

He sat down at the end of my futon, the whole thing threatening to collapse under his weight. Again, he gave the futon a disdainful look, like it had personally offended him. Even sitting down, he was huge. I'd never been very good with height estimates, but I knew he was at least 6'4, easily able to overpower my measly 5'6 form.

By this point, I was curled up in a little ball as far away as I could get without crawling up the wall.

"I could offer you the world, Emersyn," he told me, and there was power threaded through his promise, like there was no way he could break it now that he'd said it.

"I don't even know your name," I reminded him, having to force my body to not lean towards him with the way he was looking at me.

I'd never had anyone look at me like that. Like I was priceless, worthy. But here I was, in my little hovel, with a stranger looking at me like I was more priceless than gold.

"Perhaps this conversation would have turned out better if I'd led with that," he chuckled, sounding almost embarrassed. And somehow, seeing just that bit of vulnerability helped me relax just a tad.

"My name is Hendrix. I'm the Alpha of the Khan pack."

"The Khan pack?" I asked, trying to think if I'd ever heard of them before. Something niggled in the back of my brain, something important, but I couldn't quite latch on to the memory.

I shook my head. "But...why me? I'm no one. Why would you want the pack slave?"

His eyes darkened, and something red flashed within their depths. My wolf jumped inside of me, alarmed at the sight. But I blinked and whatever I'd seen was gone, the almost crystal-colored irises back.

"It's simple, really. I don't deny myself. When I see something I want, I take it."

I gritted my teeth, hating how conceited he sounded. I would always be a possession to these men, nothing but a plaything to use and discard when they were done with me.

As much as I wanted to get out of here, I wasn't going with this person. What was that saying? It was better to have the devil you knew rather than the devil you didn't? Who knew what horror would follow if I went with him.

The memory of Brayden forcing me to kiss him flickered through my head, reminding me that I actually couldn't be too sure of here either. It could always get worse.

I shook off the dark thought and belatedly realized that this stranger was softly stroking my foot, tingles emanating across my skin even from such a simple touch.

What the hell.

I yanked my foot away, and my wolf yipped inside me like she was disappointed.

"There's nothing here for you, little wolf," he murmured with a smile.

Hendrix leaned over me, his gaze licking at my skin.

"Such a pretty little wolf," he purred as his lips met mine. I moaned when he moved, but he just chuckled, enjoying torturing me as usual. His lips began to dance down my neck as I softly sighed at the perfect sensation. He made his way down to my chest, and he licked at both of my taut nipples before suckling

them gently. I moaned as one of his hands glided through my wet heat before pushing inside of me. I needed more. I wanted more. I wanted him to fill me in only the way that he could. I couldn't ever get enough of him.

He abruptly bit down on one of my nipples and my breath caught, the pain turning into pleasure like it always did.

Hendrix slid his fingers out of me and brought them to his lips, sucking on my arousal like it was candy. The sight just turned me on even more.

"Are you ready for me, little wolf?" he drawled, and I just nodded before dragging my hands through his hair and bringing his lips back to mine.

I was always ready for him. I would always want him.

What the fuck was that? I gasped as I came back to the present, painfully aware of how turned on I was. My nipples were hard points, my breathing was coming out in gasps, and I could feel the liquid heat in my underwear.

Hendrix inhaled, his eyes dilating as he took in the scent of my arousal. I was so confused...so turned on. What was going on?

"Still think it would be so bad to come with me? I could make all your fantasies become reality, sweet Emerysn," he told me, his voice even more gravel-filled with his own arousal.

"Did you do that to me?" I squeaked, wanting to either hide under a rock or jump him.

He looked at me knowingly. What kind of creature was he? I could smell wolf...but there was something more too. Something spicy and exotic that made my wolf want to howl in delight and curl up around him.

"Please leave," I begged, a tear sliding down my face in frustration that I could do nothing in this situation, nothing but beg.

"You cry so prettily," he said, cocking his head like a predator eyeing his prey. The way he said it was strange though. It wasn't done as an insult. It was like he was really admiring me.

I sniffed, but at least the weirdness of the comment made me stop crying.

"Last chance, little wolf. Are you going to come with me?" he asked, watching, fascinated as a stray, leftover tear dripped down my face.

"Do I actually have a choice?" I spit back.

He chuckled darkly before reaching into his coat and pulling out a syringe.

"What is that?" I asked, trying to scramble off the futon.

Hendrix caught me by my ankle, and the top half of me flopped to the ground so I was half on and half off the futon, struggling awkwardly to try and get away.

My wolf whined inside of me, finally a little bit worried about the situation we'd found ourselves in.

Hendrix sighed like I was seriously inconveniencing him. "I did try to do this the easy way, Emersyn," he said before stabbing the syringe into my thigh while I continued to try and get away from his iron grip.

Whatever was in that thing was strong. Within what felt like just a minute, the world started to dip and swirl around me.

"My name is Syn," I was faintly aware of saying as everything around me dimmed.

"Syn," he murmured, picking me up from my awkward position as he stroked my hair softly...almost reverently.

And then everything went black...

Beautiful trilling classical music was the first thing I heard as I came back to life. For a second, I just enjoyed the music. The notes floated over me, keeping me calm.

For a second.

Until everything that had happened came flashing into my head, making me very much aware of the pulsing migraine in my brain and the fact that I was currently in some type of vehicle...driving somewhere.

I opened my eyes and groaned as light from the window hit me in the face, making my headache worse.

There was a faint whirring sound, and then a black blind began to rise up from the window in front of me until the previously intense sunlight was barely visible.

I struggled to sit up and see what I was in. An oversized black sweatshirt had been put on me while I was out, and I was grateful for the extra coverage. I was expecting to find myself in the back of some sort of white van with my hands tied behind my back, but clearly, that wasn't the case. My hands were obviously free in front of me, and there was rich leather all around me.

Rich leather and *him*.

Hendrix was lounging to the right of me, a tablet in his lap that he was studying closely, although somehow, I knew that Hendrix was very much aware of everything that I was doing at the moment. I got the feeling he didn't miss very much.

We were in what could only be some kind of limo. I hadn't ever been in one or even seen one other than in movies or on tv shows, but the fact that the interior of the vehicle could easily hold ten people made it pretty probable.

"I thought it would be easier for you to sleep in a bigger space," commented Hendrix as I continued to study the black leather seats and the three large tv screens that were showing what looked like a constant stream of stock updates.

It took me a minute to absorb what he'd said. He'd snuck into my loft, given me some kind of wet fantasy, injected me with a drug, and then kidnapped me...and he'd wanted me to be comfortable?

I would have laughed at the ridiculousness of it all if my head hadn't hurt so bad.

"Here," he said, and I looked over to see him holding some red pills in his hand. "Painkiller," he said with a smirk that would have been sexy...if he hadn't just drugged and kidnapped me.

"I'm not taking anything from you," I said, before letting out a moan and dropping my face into my hands from the pain.

Hendrix sighed like he seemed to do quite often around me. "Syn," he said patiently.

Something fluttered inside of me at the nickname. The memory of me telling him to call me that as I was fading into fucking oblivion hit me, and I huffed and turned my head to look at him like a petulant child.

I thought I saw the ghost of a smirk, but it disappeared before I could be sure. He took a bottle of water from next to him and popped one of the red pills into his mouth before swallowing it elegantly down with water.

How did the guy make drinking water look like an art form?

He handed the rest of the pills to me. "That proves nothing," I told him stubbornly, and he lifted an eyebrow.

I was learning he wasn't a man of many words. "You could be hiding the pill in your mouth or something."

"Believe me, if I wanted to kill you, I wouldn't have gone through the effort of kidnapping you. You'll learn that I'm a very busy man, and I don't usually play with my food," he drawled.

My head felt like it was splitting in half, which was the only reason I took the pills. It was either die by headache or die by poison.

Hendrix passed me an unopened bottle of fancy-looking

water and then went back to reading whatever was on his tablet.

I popped the pills into my mouth and swallowed some of the water. The effect was almost instantaneous. Almost as soon as I swallowed them, my headache was gone, just like that.

"Fantastic, isn't it?" Hendrix mused. I looked at him in shock, but he was still studying his tablet.

"How did that work so fast?" I asked.

"It's a little something one of my doctors came up with. I like to be on the cutting edge of everything, and my clients do like their painkillers," he explained.

I looked down at the band on my wrist. Having medicine like that available would've been handy in the past. My healing didn't work like a real shifter with the bands on...speaking of bands.

"You said you could offer me the world. You could start by taking these off," I snapped, holding out my wrist.

Hendrix's eyes burned with disgust as he stared at the band.

"We'll be taking care of that as soon as we get to the compound," he said through gritted teeth. I watched in awe as razor-sharp claws extended from his hand before abruptly disappearing as he cleared his throat and seemed to get ahold of himself.

The claws had been at least five inches long. They looked like the freaking raptor claws in *Jurassic Park*. I'd never seen claws like that on a wolf shifter before.

I eyed him questioningly, but his face was perfectly blank. I'd think about that and his use of the word "compound" to describe his house later on. There was a more pressing matter...

"Why can't you take the bands off now?" I asked, and my wolf huffed in agreement with my question.

"I'm sorry, little wolf, whatever magic they used for those bands requires a witch. And I don't happen to have one of those around. I tried to take it off while you were sleeping and it zapped me. There's a witch on one of the islands nearby though. I'll have her summoned as soon as we arrive."

Before I could question him about the million things he'd just so casually mentioned, ringing filled the cabin.

Hendrix pressed a button on a panel next to him. "Is it done?" he snapped succinctly.

A chuckle filled the cabin...a sexy chuckle. Who were all these guys who managed to sound like sex when they laughed?

And what was wrong with me that I was even thinking about that?

"The deal went through. Farsi wants two thousand of the AR 500s. He barely blinked at the price."

"Excellent. Leak news of the purchase to our old friend. Then call the Russians. Tell them they'll be needing the ARs shortly, and double the price. Lev won't hesitate after he hears about Farsi's purchase."

My mind was whirling. AR 500s were guns. Fancy guns, if I was remembering correctly. Anton was a collector of weaponry, and I knew he had that one displayed in his office with a million sensors surrounding it just in case someone wanted to steal it. What was this talk of Russians though? What did this guy do for a living?

Looking around, it was obvious that he was wealthy. This limo was even fancier than anything I'd seen in the movies, and staring at Hendrix in the daylight made it clear that everything about him just screamed wealth. He was wearing a black button-down shirt, made of a super shiny material that looked so soft I was almost tempted to touch it. The shirt was unbuttoned to show off the top of his sculpted chest, of course. Because the eye candy on his face wasn't enough, apparently.

He had to have what looked like a fantastic drool-worthy body too.

"I'd advise you to stop looking at me like that," Hendrix growled, and I realized that the call had ended and he'd caught me drooling over him.

"I wasn't looking at you like anything," I told him, and this time it wasn't a hint of a grin that I got, but a full-fledged smile that almost made me gasp. It transformed him from beautiful...to otherworldly.

I turned my attention to the window on the other side of me because I knew there was no way I could hide the effect he'd had on me with that smile.

"Wow," I murmured as I looked out, and I leaned closer, trying to see through the screen he'd put up earlier to block out the sun.

The ocean was out there. The screen began to retract, giving me a clear look at a view I never thought I'd see. The Hallow Sector had been barren, ugly...dry. I'd kind of thought that it was a fitting landscape for the state of my life. I'd heard that the ocean was only a few hours away, but it might as well have been on the other side of the world.

My wolf circled around inside of me, just as delighted about the view. If Hendrix was telling the truth, and he actually got these bands off of me...well, I knew my wolf would be just as excited as me about that. I could tell she was already picturing running in the sand and jumping in the waves.

I'd always been a big reader. With all the medical procedures after the fire, I'd gotten really behind in school, and no one had bothered to help me catch up. So I read. There was a small library in the town that hardly anyone used, and whenever I got breaks I would sneak over there. They didn't get new books very often, so I'd gone through all the books in the building several times, but it had been my escape, the only time I could see the world.

For some reason, there had been a whole aquatic section in the library, a little strange for a town located in a desert-type climate. For a while, I'd been obsessed with reading everything that I could about the ocean. I'd gotten lost in the pages of *Treasure Island*, learned all about Great White Sharks, and gone *20,000 Leagues Under the Sea*.

But I never thought I would get to see the ocean in person.

I watched in awe as the waves lapped against the sandy shore. Families were playing on the beach, girls laying out under the sun, and surfers cresting the waves in the distance. The water was a light blue color, so light it reminded me of Hendrix's eyes.

Not that I was thinking about his eyes.

I turned to see that he was watching me way too knowingly, like he could see everything that was in my head, see the desperation I'd felt for so many years being trapped in that place.

"You mentioned that the witch lived on a nearby island. Does that mean you live on an island?" I asked quietly, trying to hold in how excited the thought made me.

He nodded, his gaze trailing across my features thoughtfully as if he'd just come up with a plan. "We own several islands. Our main compound is located on the largest one, but we have people and different businesses that live on the others."

A wave of exhilaration passed through me. Even if I was trading one prison for another, at least there would be a better view.

That was, if they kept me alive.

I turned my gaze back to the beautiful scenery, going over everything that I knew about Hendrix so far.

Still a whole lot of nothing.

"Have you ever been out of the Hallow Sector?" Hendrix asked. I glanced at him. He was typing away on his tablet.

"No. I haven't. But I always...wanted to."

"Hmmm.." he said, without adding anything else.

I sighed as I went back to the pretty views, neither of us saying a word. I tried to keep my eyes open, but the gentle purring of the car, combined with the classical music that was still drifting through the speakers, soon pushed me gently into dreamland.

"Little wolf," I faintly heard Hendrix murmur as something touched my cheek, caressing it before moving away. I opened my eyes and soon realized that we'd come to a stop. The door closest to Hendrix in the vehicle was open.

"What are we doing?" I asked, instantly going on alert. Somehow he'd managed to lull me into a small sense of security while on the drive, but I was on edge now.

"I have some business to attend to before we make it back to my home. We're going to switch transportation so we get there faster," Hendrix said matter of factly before he gracefully stepped out of the vehicle.

My stomach chose that moment to growl loudly, and I winced at my stiff muscles as I slid out of the car as well, doing it very *un*gracefully.

I sighed in pleasure as I inhaled the salty air. Even though I knew I must have slept for a while, judging by how much lower the sun was in the sky, we were still by the sea.

A breeze brushed across my face, and I had to resist the urge to dance around in glee at the sensation.

The air in the Hallow Sector was always bitingly hot, drying out your eyes and your skin and adding to the desolate feel of the place. Wherever we were now was doing the opposite. My wolf was practically doing somersaults inside of me.

"I'm thinking you won't have a problem with the climate," Hendrix mused, and I realized that he was standing there watching me. I grimaced in embarrassment. Who knows what giddy, goofy expression I'd had splashed across my face just from breathing in air.

But it was really good air.

Just then, I bothered to look beyond him where I could see a giant black plane. Men and women were hustling in and out of the plane, loaded down with bags and boxes. There was a strange red eternity-looking symbol near the back tail section.

My stomach growled again.

"Come on, little wolf. There will be a meal prepared for us on the plane."

I shifted uncomfortably, half tempted to jump back into the limo even though I had no idea how to drive.

"Is that thing safe?" I blurted out, a little squeak in my voice as I stared at the plane, images of it falling to the ground in a fiery blaze filling my head.

I shivered and noted the small grin of his that appeared and disappeared on the asshole's face again.

"It's my personal plane, so it's the very best," he said simply, like that was explanation enough.

Knowing I didn't have a choice, and wanting to walk rather than be forced on, I reluctantly let go of the door and made my way over to him.

His hand went to my lower back, and tingles sprinted out across my skin from his touch. He wasn't touching me through the sweatshirt, but his hand was in that hollow space, right above my butt, and it felt so proprietary...so intimate. I stiffened, but he either didn't notice or was pretending not to because he didn't move his hand the entire walk from the car to the plane.

I'd felt deep feelings towards Brayden, the Moon Goddess ensured that. But this spark, this feeling that every touch from Hendrix could swallow me whole...I'd never felt that with Brayden.

It was very confusing...and alarming.

There were two scary-looking men stationed at the base of the stairs that led into the plane, and Hendrix nodded at them in acknowledgment but didn't say anything.

I walked like an unsteady colt up the steps, very aware of Hendrix's presence right behind me...I swore I could feel his gaze centered on my ass...and stepped right into another luxurious world.

There were a few people already on the large plane, but they weirdly kept their eyes averted from me like I didn't exist. I didn't know whether to feel relieved or annoyed about that, but I didn't think about it for too long. I was too caught up staring at everything.

This plane wasn't some small prop plane. It was a full-on jet that could have seated at least a hundred people if the interior had been situated differently. And everything was in black and red.

There were different seating areas filled with a mix of comfy-looking sofas and armchairs. A few actual airplane seats like I'd seen on TV were sprinkled here and there, I guess in case you actually needed to buckle up. Large-screen TVs were everywhere, all playing a mixture of the same stock and news channels that had been playing in the limo. Some of the people were studiously watching the screens, typing things down on tablets in their laps every so often. I could see at least three doors towards the back of the plane, and I suspected there were probably rooms back there like I'd read about in books.

An image of a black silk bed flickered through my brain... but I quickly pushed that away.

Hendrix didn't talk to anyone as he led me towards the back. There had been three men in suits working on a sectional couch, but when they saw Hendrix heading towards them, they jumped up and fled.

It was a little odd to see grown men looking like they were going to pee their pants in fear, but Hendrix didn't seem to see anything strange about it because he continued to lead me right towards the couch that they'd just abandoned and motioned for me to sit down.

I sighed as soon as my butt hit the couch. I'd never felt anything so comfy in my life. I leaned back into the cushion, studying everything around me.

A gorgeous woman dressed in a tight black skirt and red silk blouse popped up and walked over to us, her gaze locked eagerly on Hendrix. If she wasn't careful, she was going to drool all over her shirt.

"What can I get you, sir?" she purred, her voice coming out so sexual that I shifted awkwardly in my seat, wondering if she was about to try and climb into his lap.

A rush of something unfamiliar slid through me. My wolf didn't like this girl standing so close to Hendrix, especially acting like that.

I didn't particularly like it either.

Just another thing I was going to studiously ignore about my interactions with Hendrix.

"Two filets, asparagus, and the au gratin potatoes," Hendrix ordered, not even bothering to look at her. My wolf was slightly mollified by that and backed down enough that I stopped feeling like I was going to leap at the girl.

"And drinks?" she asked, a bit of hurt creeping into her voice as she finally turned her attention to me with a frown.

Hendrix looked over at me, his hand finding my knee as

his thumb made small movements across my skin. I couldn't withhold the shiver this time as our gazes met.

"Water's good," I said in a raspy voice.

Hendrix licked his bottom lip sensually, and I felt like a fly caught in a spider's web as we continued to stare at each other. Did Stockholm Syndrome usually happen this fast? Because this was something.

"Two waters and a scotch," Hendrix ordered, finally sparing the girl a glance. Her face brightened like she was expecting him to suddenly fall at her feet in love. Instead, he said, "that's all," and looked down at the tablet he'd pulled out, still keeping one hand on my knee.

She shot me a dark look, like she wanted to kill me, and then stalked away, garnering plenty of looks from the other males on the plane...but obviously not from the one she wanted.

I guess I could just hope that she didn't spit in my food.

"All of these people work for you?" I asked as the door at the front of the cabin was closed and the plane's engines began to roar. My fingers dug into the couch cushion as I looked longingly at one of the cabin chairs up ahead that had a seatbelt.

As a shifter, it was hard to kill me, even with the bands around my wrist keeping my wolf imprisoned, but I was pretty sure that a plane crash could do it.

The girl returned with a tray carrying the drinks. There was a black marble-looking coffee table in front of us, and she carefully set down the drinks without spilling a drop before walking away without a word.

I picked up the water, eyeing it carefully to make sure I didn't see anything resembling spit.

"She wouldn't dare to do something to your drink. Merideth obviously thinks that a few fucks should give her special attention. Something she will quickly learn does not."

"You've slept with her?" I asked, my voice sounding way too interested.

He cocked his head, that sly smile of his sliding across his face. "A few times here and there on long flights. Does that bother you, little wolf?"

I rolled my eyes and took a big gulp of my water, almost choking myself in the process.

The plane began to move, and I flinched and set down my water, forgetting all about Hendrix and the girl as butterflies began to swarm in my stomach.

"Drink this," Hendrix said gruffly, picking up the scotch and handing it to me. I drank it back without question, desperate for some liquid courage.

The butterflies turned into bats as the plane ascended into the air, and I went from gripping onto the couch to gripping onto Hendrix's leg like it could somehow keep me safe.

"Deep breaths, little wolf," Hendrix murmured, stroking my hair softly.

My breaths were more like gulps of air as I closed my eyes and tried to think happy thoughts.

I just didn't have a lot of happy thoughts to draw from, so it wasn't a huge success.

The plane leveled off, and I was finally able to breathe normally right as Merideth arrived with two plates of food that even smelled heavenly after the panic attack I'd just experienced.

She set the plates down on the coffee table with rolled-up silverware before standing up and pointedly staring at where my hand was still holding onto Hendrix's leg.

I hastily let him go...which did not make Hendrix happy.

"Do you have a problem, Merideth?" he asked silkily, the danger in his voice so obvious that I was suddenly scared for her.

"N-no sir," she said, her face paling. Merideth took a deep

gulp and then pushed back a lock of her pretty brown hair. "But if we could talk for a moment privately," she stupidly continued.

"There is nothing you could possibly have to say to me except 'yes sir,' and 'do you need anything else?' Is that clear?" he said coldly, his eyes beginning to flash red like they had the night before.

A sob tore out of Merideth's throat, and she scampered away as fast she could.

"Christopher," Hendrix called mildly in only a slightly elevated voice.

As if he had been waiting to be called, which I suspected he had been, a nervous-looking guy dressed in a sharp grey suit leaped from a couch a few feet away and hustled over. "Yes, sir?"

"Make sure Merideth is reassigned to one of the outer islands. I don't want to see her again."

If Christopher thought that was an odd request, he didn't show it. "Of course, sir. I'll put her on a different flight back on our next stop." He bowed slightly to both of us and then hustled back to his seat where he resumed studying a screen filled with scrolling stocks.

"Eat," Hendrix ordered as he picked up one of the plates and handed it to me.

I found myself shoveling in some of the potatoes and almost orgasming right there because I'd never tasted anything so good in my life. I hadn't gotten any kind of income for my work at the bar. Someone had delivered some ramen and canned goods to my loft once a week. It had been tasteless, but it had kept me alive. What I was tasting right now was so beyond anything I remembered in my life that it honestly had me second-guessing this whole kidnapping thing.

I'd seen the ocean and was eating steak straight from the Moon Goddess herself.

When was the shoe going to drop?

I didn't speak again until I'd completely demolished my plate, and Hendrix wisely kept silent as he ate his own meal.

When I felt like my stomach was in danger of exploding, I finally set down my fork.

"Does everyone always listen to everything you say?" I asked, studying how everyone in the plane was working and shooting panicked glances at Hendrix every time he moved.

"Yes," he drawled, leaning back into the sofa, clearly amused.

"Do you ever get tired of it?" I asked, not sure why I was brave enough to ask all these questions, but figuring I had nothing to lose.

All amusement fled his face and he leaned forward. "You should know better than most, little wolf. Once you've lived life as an ant, you'll do whatever it takes to never be an ant again."

I had a million questions, but I held my tongue. There was a haunted, fierce look in his eyes, and at that moment I decided it was best to stay as far away from his demons as possible.

I had enough of my own.

The rest of the flight passed without incident. Hendrix worked the whole time, and I stared out the window at the passing clouds...and napped. Apparently, Hendrix had that effect on me.

I was relaxed enough that I barely sweated as the plane touched down. Hendrix pulled me up and guided me towards the front as soon as the plane door opened. Everyone else stayed seated until we'd passed. I took one step outside and promptly gasped, knowing exactly where we were.

Fervian City.

Fervian City was home to the rich and famous of the

world. A place that had always seemed more like a story from a fairy tale than a real place.

But here we were.

Tall, gleaming skyscrapers stretched high in the sky. Luxury cars moved down the golden-colored streets, and beautiful people were everywhere.

I'd been surrounded by luxury for several hours now, but it still struck me how strange the world was that some people had so much...and some people had so little.

"Come on, little wolf," Hendrix said, gently moving me forward so that I would go down the stairs. There was a shiny black town car waiting a few feet away, and I hurried down the stairs, assuming we would be getting in that.

I slowed when I saw all of the men strapped down with machine guns standing around watching our surroundings closely, like any minute we were going to come under attack.

Evidently, this was par for the course for Hendrix, because he simply put his hand on my lower back and pushed me towards the town car as if the armed men didn't exist at all.

"What did you say you did again?" I asked as I slid into the car's over-the-top cream leather interior.

Hendrix chuckled darkly. "I don't think I said," he responded as the driver started the car and began to pull away without a word from Hendrix.

He was obviously being deliberately obtuse.

"Well, do you think you could enlighten me? There were a lot of guns out there. Are you expecting an attack?"

Hendrix was already back to typing on his tablet. I was learning he was never far from either that or his phone.

"I provide assets to countries all over the world. And sometimes, that makes me a target," he explained calmly.

I shot a nervous look at the driver since it was obvious that Hendrix's business wasn't exactly on the up and up.

"Everyone that works for me knows exactly who I am and

what I'm capable of," he said in answer to my questioning look.

I bit my lip. "What kind of assets are we talking about?" I pressed.

Hendrix cocked an eyebrow. "Are you sure you want to know the answer to that? Once you open that door, there's no going back."

"Are you planning on eventually letting me go?" I asked, a little too excitedly.

That terrifying red gleam that I was now confident was not a figment of my imagination came to the surface of Hendrix's gaze. "I won't ever be letting you go," he said fervently.

I hadn't really been expecting any other answer, but the news was still depressing. My wolf was excited about the prospect of staying with Hendrix forever though. She was practically dancing around inside of me. She and I really needed to have a talk about her taste in men.

"Will you tell me then, if there's no chance of me getting away?" I asked, feeling desperate for the information even though I knew it wasn't going to be good.

"I'm an arms dealer, little wolf. I create, trade, and sell weapons of all kinds to my buyers. I also have a branch of my business that exchanges protection to shifter communities for payment. But obviously, that business doesn't compare to my weapons empire."

My heart skipped in alarm. "By customers around the world, do you mean countries?" I asked, feeling more scared by the second.

"Countries, kingdoms, interest groups... I'll sell to anyone for the right price," he answered, obviously amused.

"Interest groups? Like... terrorist groups?" I clarified softly.

"I don't subscribe to traditional terms. I answer to money and that's it. I don't care about the political happenings of the world. I only care about myself—and my brothers, I suppose," he added almost reluctantly.

"Are you scared now?" he asked, the idea of my fear seeming to excite him.

"I would be a fool not to be," I said softly.

"What's the matter, little wolf? Have you never craved excitement? We both know that your life was going nowhere in that pack. It was only a matter of time before you would be sent to Reject Island. You should be thanking me," he told me.

I stiffened, inane shame washing over me. For some reason, I hadn't thought that he was aware of my sordid history. But of course, he was. He'd known about the bands around my wrist, hadn't he? I hadn't done anything wrong in what happened between Brayden and myself, but there was a certain shame that felt impossible to get rid of now that I had been rejected by the only person in the world that the Moon Goddess had determined was my perfect fit. There was also the fact that Brayden was terrible, a truly disgusting shifter. What did that say about me, that she thought he'd be my ideal mate?

"So you know everything?" I asked softly as we passed rows and rows of luxury brand stores. I stared at them, not really taking anything in, but I couldn't look at him. What was he thinking right now?

There was a long silence, but he finally answered.

"I always do research before my acquisitions," he said, and for some reason, some stupid reason, the word 'acquisition' burned in my chest.

My biggest mistake in all of this would be ever thinking that I was more than that.

All of the glitter of Hendrix's world was dangerous, momentarily distracting from the situation I found myself in.

A screen suddenly began to rise between where the driver was sitting and where we were seated. I looked over at Hendrix questioningly, but he didn't say anything until the screen was all the way up. With his right hand still holding his beloved tablet, his left hand was clenching open and closed, like he was trying to ease some tension.

"I read about your father," he commented softly, and my breath hitched. You would think that the years would have made the pain fade, but every time I thought about that night, every time I thought about waking up and finding out that Jamie was dead, my heart still felt like it was being torn apart.

"My father was a terrible man, too," he said quietly.

My eyes widened, but I stayed quiet, hoping that he would tell me more. When you saw a man like Hendrix, who seemed to own the very air that you breathed, it was hard to believe that we could share similar pasts. It was almost more depressing, actually, if that were the case. Because while he obviously rose up from the ashes, I'd stayed laying in them.

"He was mentally unstable, heard voices in his head. And one day he took the three of us to the lake and tried to drown us. He told the authorities he was 'getting rid of our demons'," Hendrix chuckled darkly as he stared blankly at his lap, obviously caught in memories of the past. "Little did he know, he actually created three demons that day."

I shivered at his words.

"Where was your mother?" I asked tentatively.

"We had been told that she left. Ran away and left us behind. But I doubt that's true. I'm sure she's lying in a shallow grave somewhere, a victim of my father's insanity," he responded blankly.

Damn him. Damn him all to hell. Here I was trying to remember my place in this new world, and he was making me *feel*. I hadn't met a lot of people with tragic backstories. Not that most of my pack hadn't been tragic in general, they just hadn't had the horror laced into their backstory like I did.

Before he could say anything, the town car came to a stop.

I peered out the window, seeing nothing but the glittering skyscrapers, no clue of where we were, or what we were doing.

The driver was suddenly at my door, opening it for me. I paused for a second getting out, wondering if I could break away and disappear into the crowds on the sidewalk, but my wolf barked at me before I could come up with any concrete plan.

"Syn," Hendrix said in warning, like he could read my mind.

I gave up my thoughts on running and allowed the driver to escort me to the sidewalk where Hendrix was waiting.

He yanked me closer to him, and a low growl broke from his throat. At first, I thought he was growling at me, and then I realized that his growl was focused on the deathly white driver who was backing away slowly with his hands in the air beseechingly. "Mine," he growled in warning. "Don't ever touch her."

"Yes, sir," the driver responded in a trembling voice as he practically dashed back to the other side of the vehicle and jumped into the town car.

My mouth opened and closed, but then Hendrix's arm wasn't just resting on my back—it was wrapped around me, pulling me to his side so that I was nestled against him, unable to escape the delicious scent of him. My wolf moaned, wanting more. I was too shocked to do anything.

"Not my girl," he murmured into my hair, as his hand massaged the side of my waist like he was reassuring himself that I was still there. "There's nowhere that you could run where I wouldn't find you, little wolf," he promised.

I shivered, wondering why the threat sounded so comforting.

He led me through an impressive set of gold and glass doors, and I lost all train of thought.

We were in an aquatic wonderland. Straight ahead of us

was an enormous fish tank that stretched across the entire large room and at least five stories up. I watched in shock and awe as a huge 15-foot shark came into view, looking like it was headed straight towards the glass before it abruptly turned and swam away. Fish in every color under the rainbow flitted in and out of elaborate coral and rock structures. Enormous manta rays, as big as I was, swam in and out of view. It was incredible. As a child, I remembered going to a nearby aquarium as part of the class school trip before everything had gone to hell, of course. But the tanks in that place didn't even come close to rivaling what I was seeing in front of me.

After staring at it for a long moment, only then did I become aware of the sharply dressed men and women milling around, holding exotic-looking drinks in long stem flutes as they admired the view in front of them and talked and laughed with each other.

"What is this place?" I asked in amazement, turning my attention reluctantly away from the aquarium to look at Hendrix.

To my surprise, he wasn't looking at the sight in front of him. He was staring down at my face, a golden light in his eyes, like the amazing sight wasn't the tank in front of us...it was me.

"One of the most famous restaurant/event centers in the world. People come from all over to see the wonders housed in this building."

Restaurant and event centers? Looking around, I noticed that the people in the room weren't just well dressed, they were *very* well dressed. I was suddenly aware of the fact that I was still in an oversized sweatshirt and my tiny pair of pajama shorts, along with a pair of flip-flops. Not sure how I'd forgotten that fact. People were shooting us looks, or maybe they were just shooting Hendrix looks. There was fear and respect in their gazes, and it became very clear that almost all of them knew who he was.

As usual, Hendrix didn't seem to care about anyone else in the room, nor was he even aware that they were here at all. Still holding onto me tightly, he led me over to the side of the room where a gorgeous blonde-haired woman sheathed in a sparkling silver dress was waiting behind a maître d' stand.

"Everything is ready, sir," she said quickly, before Hendrix had even said a word. "Right this way," she told us, gesturing to the glass door that was sliding open behind her.

We followed her through the doors, and I found myself in a long hallway, a glass wall to the left holding another tank that stretched from floor to ceiling and spanning the entire length of the hallway. Hendrix had to practically drag me along behind the woman because I was so caught up in watching three dolphins swim around and play with each other. "Those are dolphins," I squealed, unable to contain my excitement. Hendrix's hand briefly tightened on my hip in response, but he didn't say anything.

At the end of the long hallway was another set of sliding glass doors, and I reluctantly allowed Hendrix to lead me away from the tank and into the next room.

The new room held another set of wonders, except this time it came in the form of gorgeous dresses. There were racks and racks of gowns in all different colors, and in all different fabrics and lengths. The woman bowed low to us before disappearing from the room without another word.

No sooner had she disappeared, than a woman with a sharp, severe black bob, red lipstick, and a fitted black tux came into view. She was the most bad-ass looking woman I'd ever seen. She gave a sharp nod to Hendrix before eyeing me critically.

"I think my selections will work," she said in a lilting accent that I couldn't place as she nodded to herself.

Before I could ask what "selections" she was talking about, she pulled out a measuring tape and walked towards me.

Hendrix let out a sharp growl again, and the woman and I both jumped. She quickly stepped back from me and looked at Hendrix apologetically. "Just need to take some measurements. May I, sir?" she asked, pausing in her ministrations.

"Do it without touching her," he ordered, and the woman nodded like there was nothing out of the ordinary or crazy with that statement.

Hendrix was acting very...possessive. I wasn't sure what to make of that.

The woman began to measure me all over, making sure that she never touched me. It was quite an uncomfortable experience, especially because I didn't know the woman's name.

"I'm Syn," I told her as she was measuring my ass. The woman didn't pause.

"Jacqueline," she answered in a stiff, cool voice.

She didn't say anything else, and I didn't press her for conversation. After all, what would I say? Oh hey, I've been kidnapped. How's your life going?

Jacqueline finished measuring me and then hustled to the other side of the room, disappearing behind some racks of dresses.

"Are you going to tell me what we're doing here?" I asked Hendrix, who was staring avidly at his phone, typing furiously away.

"Just dinner, little wolf," he said. And of course, at that moment, my stomach decided to growl. Despite the fact that the steak we'd had on the plane had been the most delicious thing I'd ever tasted, it had been several hours since then, and with my adrenaline in a constant high with all of the new things happening, I was starving again.

My wolf yipped inside of me. Evidently, she was hungry as well.

Jacqueline came back into the room pushing a clothing rack. The entire rack was filled with clothes. She pulled out a plum-colored gown with a plunging neckline and started to hand it to me.

"The silver one," Hendrix barked, and Jacqueline froze.

She quickly put the dress back and grabbed a sparkling silver dress completely encrusted with crystals. It looked like it was the size of my left toe though, and I eyed it incredulously as she brought it to me.

"What do you think?" she asked in that pretty accent of hers. But she wasn't asking me, she was asking Hendrix.

I was so overwhelmed by everything that was happening, I was only faintly annoyed by the fact that I was being ignored.

"That's the one," he said, and she nodded subserviently before gesturing towards a door to the left of us. She walked towards the door, her heels clicking against the marble tile, and opened it up to reveal a luxurious dressing room.

But it wasn't a normal dressing room—this one held a shower, a velvet-looking bench, and a mirrored station that held an assortment of different cosmetics.

When I didn't move to follow her, she huffed in annoyance. "Your reservation is in thirty minutes. Please come in."

I hustled after her, still confused about what was going on.

"Let me know if you need anything," she said succinctly before exiting the room and closing the door behind her.

I was feeling very much like a fish out of water, pun intended, considering the surroundings, but I decided that a shower would be nice. Getting kidnapped wasn't exactly a sweat-proof activity.

It took me about five minutes to figure out how to turn on the thing, but once I did, it was worth it. Three nozzles were going at once, one consisting of a waterfall spray that came straight down from the ceiling. The water was the perfect temperature, and there were at least 10 bottles of shampoos and body washes available for me to use with complimentary vanilla and coconut scents that almost had my eyes rolling to the back of my head with how good they smelled. I could have stayed in the shower forever, but I eventually turned it off and made use of a large, fluffy towel that had been on a heating rack right outside the shower. Because of course, you couldn't use a non-heated towel in a place like this.

After wrapping the towel around me, I stared down at the cosmetics in dismay before deciding to dry my hair first since I actually knew how to do that. I was out of practice using makeup since I hadn't had an excess of funds to blow on making myself pretty.

Blow drying took only a few minutes thanks to whatever high-tech ability the blow dryer had. My hair looked like silk after I was finished, and I couldn't help but admire it, even with my scars marring the view from the back.

The scars. Hendrix just had this effect on me, where I forgot myself. He wouldn't have seen the scars last night in the dark, but he would have for sure seen them when he put on the sweatshirt. Yet he hadn't said anything. And even if he somehow missed it while putting on the sweatshirt, he would have heard about them when he heard about my family.

Trying to push that little fact out of my mind, I decided to put on the dress next. I eyed it incredulously for a long minute. It was so pretty, but it really was so small. Thinking that I at least needed to attempt to try it on, I picked it up and pushed it over my head before trying to pull it down my body. I squeezed and sucked in, and I somehow got the dress all the way down. It was skin-tight, but staring in the mirror, it looked like it had been made for me. I was...pretty. Not a thought that I'd had much before in my life. The dress fell all the way to the floor, and it was high enough in the back that only a little of the scarring peeked out.

Not that there's anything to be ashamed of, I reminded myself as my wolf huffed in agreement.

The dress had tiny cap sleeves and dipped low enough to tastefully show my cleavage. I couldn't have dreamt up a prettier piece of clothing.

Deciding that the dress deserved a little bit of makeup, I fumbled through the packages on the makeup stand until I came across some mascara, blush, and lipstick. I at least knew how to do that. The pink lipstick that I tried on somehow didn't seem to fit my new look, and I debated for a long minute before grabbing the red lipstick and carefully putting it on. Before I could spend any more time admiring myself though, the door practically crashed open as Jacqueline all but stormed in.

"Very good," she said in surprise, and it honestly felt like the nicest compliment I'd ever had. She held up a pair of sparkling silver high heels and gestured for me to put them on. I slid them on and then attempted to walk a few steps, feeling like a newborn foal as I did so.

Jacqueline sighed in annoyance before reaching over to a box I hadn't noticed on the bench and revealing a pair of kitten-heeled silver sandals that would be much easier to walk in.

"Thank you," I told her as I slid off the high heels and slipped the sandals on. Much better.

"Time to go, Cinderella," she said, just the corner of her lip tipping up in amusement. I snorted, not sure that the description was accurate, before taking a deep breath and heading out to where Hendrix was waiting. His back was turned to us, and he was rifling through some clothes, an enormous pile stacking up next to him. For a second, a flicker of what could have been jealousy passed through me as I wondered who those clothes were for, but I pushed the feeling away. Although, if someone claimed to own you, you really should be able to own them right back.

Not that I had an interest in owning Hendrix.

My wolf snorted in disagreement.

Hendrix heard my steps and turned around. When he saw me, his face went totally blank, nothing but a tic in his cheek showing. I shifted uncomfortably, smoothing down the front of my dress nervously. Did he hate it? And why the hell did I even care?

"You look exquisite," he finally said hoarsely, and I was faintly aware of Jacqueline giving a sigh of relief from somewhere behind me. "Hopefully everyone has enough self-preservation to keep their eyeballs," he muttered slowly, and Jacqueline giggled nervously.

I blushed under his stare before noticing that he had changed. He was dressed in a classic black and white tux, no bowtie or tie. Instead, he had the first couple of buttons undone like he had earlier, and I found my mouth watering at the sight of his smooth, tan skin. Was it weird to be attracted to someone's neck?

He strode over to me and grabbed the back of my neck firmly with one hand, smoothing the skin softly with his thumb as he looked down at me. Something fluttered in my chest...dangerously close to my heart. He was standing so close. Was he going to...

"I'll take those, make sure that they all have the right measurements," Hendrix ordered, snapping me out of the spell he'd put me under.

I looked over his shoulder. "Are those for..." I began.

"You'll need clothes, won't you?" he asked. I nodded, my mouth flopping open like a fish as Jacqueline hustled by us and grabbed the stack.

Hendrix abruptly let me go and then put an arm around

my waist before leading me back out the door that we had first come in.

"Thank you," I threw over my shoulder, feeling awkward about just walking away.

Jacqueline didn't respond. She was probably too busy adding up all the dollar bills she would get from her commission.

A man was waiting for us right outside, and his eyes widened when he saw us.

"Eyes down," snapped Hendrix, and the poor guy not only looked down at the ground but also turned completely around so he couldn't see us at all.

"Is that really necessary?" I muttered under my breath, and Hendrix growled and pulled me closer.

"Every person in the building is going to want you before the night is up. I'm thinking it's very necessary."

They haven't seen my scars, was the first thing I thought as we walked behind the practically quivering man. I thought about Brayden's face when he'd seen them for the first time that night, the disgust in his gaze. *"Such a pity," he'd whispered.*

"What are you thinking about right now?" Hendrix asked, knocking me out of the past.

"Nothing," I responded quickly. He'd already seen me way too vulnerable as it was. I didn't want to give him even more ammunition to decide I was pathetic.

He stopped suddenly, and I almost fell over. He gripped my neck softly but firmly, his thumb rubbing across my pulse. His eyes were glowing red as he stared at me. "Don't lie to me, Emersyn. Ever," he said sternly.

He let go abruptly and started moving me forward without saying anything else.

We walked down a nondescript hallway before stopping at a door.

"Enjoy your night, sir and madam," the guy said, giving an awkward bow before quickly striding away.

The door in front of us slid open just then, and I let out a loud gasp. In front of us, there was a tunnel completely surrounded by water and swimming sea creatures. Beyond the tunnel was a room, also surrounded on all sides by water, with a dining table and chairs set up.

"This has to be a dream," I murmured, and Hendrix laughed. It was a real laugh, not just a chuckle. When I looked at him, surprised at the sound, I saw that he looked just as surprised as I was to have laughed.

He shook his head, confusion in his gaze before leading me through the tunnel and into the room. There was another clear tunnel on top of the room that led straight up.

I wandered around the room, realizing whatever giant tank surrounded us was a shark tank and there were hundreds of sharks swimming around everywhere.

It was incredible.

"Hold on," Hendrix said suddenly, and I looked at him questioningly right before the room started to move. It went up the tunnel, and I realized that the floor was also completely clear. As we moved higher, it really felt like we were immersed completely on all sides by water.

Staring at everything, I began to feel emotional.

"Why are you showing me all of this?" I asked him. Like when we'd first walked into this place, he was spending more time watching me than watching the underwater kingdom around us.

For the first time since I'd met him, a flicker of insecurity flashed across his face. Of course, it was gone in an instant, but still...I'd seen it.

"I—want you to be happy," he said haltingly. "You said you hadn't ever seen the world. So this was the start of me showing it to you."

I had the urge to cry because it was the nicest sentiment I'd heard in a very long time, but at the same time...how could I trust it? He'd still kidnapped me. He'd still injected me with a drug when I refused to cooperate.

But... Nope, I was going to stand strong. I wasn't going there.

"Shall we eat?" Hendrix asked, clearly noticing my internal debate.

"That sounds great," I answered softly, feeling unsure.

Hendrix pulled out a chair for me, and I settled into it, wondering where the food was. Before I could ask, he sat down and pressed a small button on the table I hadn't noticed. To my shock, the middle of the table opened up and a tray floated up, loaded down with delicious smelling food.

A hammerhead shark chose that moment to swim by, and I shook my head and giggled, overwhelmed with how surreal the moment was.

The meal was a variety of Asian dishes, and I didn't even try to be ladylike to match the setting as I loaded my plate and my mouth down with noodles, orange chicken, fried rice, and egg rolls. We ate mostly in silence, but it wasn't awkward. We both were watching the scene that surrounded us, and occasionally we would both point out things we saw.

"What's your home like?" I asked finally, wanting to take advantage of his good mood.

He bit his bottom lip as he thought, and I shifted in my seat, finding it much too sexy.

"It's different from the other shifter islands. It's farther south, so we get much warmer temperatures than they do up north. I've never been one for the cold. We're self-sustaining, so when we trade, it's only to buy specialty items, but we can produce almost anything ourselves."

"All from just one small island?" I asked, leaning towards him as I tried to envision it as he spoke.

He grinned cockily. "We actually own multiple large islands—five, in fact. We have staff on every island in charge of different crops and livestock. There is also a ring of smaller islands around the main ones that we use for security posts."

I was still absorbing the fact that the man in front of me owned that many islands, but his mention of security snagged my attention. "Security posts?"

"By nature of my job, I've made a lot of...enemies. Or at least people that are looking for any way to dismantle my organization." He shrugs as if the prospect of that is nothing. "Our security ensures that doesn't become an issue."

I nodded thoughtfully, trying to imagine what my new home was like as we continued eating.

The meal was by far one of the most, if not the most, perfect moments of my life.

Too bad it couldn't last.

After we finished, Hendrix glanced down at his watch and frowned. "It's time for my meeting, unfortunately, but have you enjoyed your meal?"

"It's been incredible," I told him sincerely, and his gaze softened as he watched me.

"I meant what I said, little wolf. I want you to be happy in this new life. I'll make sure you are."

I blushed, ignoring the urging from my wolf to jump across the table and kiss him. Hendrix cleared his throat, his gaze filled with promises that I was finding I very much wanted to come true.

He hummed as he held my gaze and then stood up, rolling his shoulders back like he was trying to shake off the intimate moment. He pressed the same button on the table that had brought up the food, but this time it began to lower us back down from where we'd come from. My stomach dipped, a certain wave of apprehension passing over me for no apparent reason.

Once we'd returned to the bottom of the tunnel, Hendrix led me out of the aquatic wonder, and after turning down two hallways, we walked back outside without seeing anyone. It was night time and the street was lit up, the sound of laughter filling the air from passersby going in and out of the restaurants and bars along the street.

A car was waiting for us outside the entrance even though it was different from the one we'd used to go inside. I hadn't seen him use his phone since before dinner, and I was once again impressed with how perfectly orchestrated his life was. All of his employees seemed to know exactly what he wanted before it even happened. I'm sure there was a high level of planning involved behind the scenes, but still, it was all very impressive.

We got back into the town car, but this time, other than the same driver from before, there was a new man was sitting in the passenger seat, one I hadn't seen before. He looked back at Hendrix, keeping his gaze carefully averted from me, and nodded respectfully. The man was tall, so tall that his head almost hit the top of the car. He had a bulbous nose and strong lips, the kind of face you didn't forget just because it was so unique.

"Everything's ready. All the lines have been diverted and the crew is in place for clean-up. There shouldn't be any issues," the man said.

"Good. I want this to be quick," Hendrix responded as the driver pulled the car away from the curb and we set off down the road. No one bothered to introduce the man to me, and he and Hendrix chatted about various stocks and trades that had happened that day. I tried to listen to get a glimpse of Hendrix's businesses, but a lot of the terms were way over my head. I definitely hadn't come across any books on these subjects in the town library.

I shifted uncomfortably in my seat and then Hendrix's

hand was suddenly on my knee, stroking it, even though his attention never left the man in the front seat. A warm feeling flooded over me, and again, I tried to ignore it. It didn't make him a saint that he'd thrown me an ounce of kindness today.

My wolf huffed in disagreement and urged me to cuddle up next to Hendrix, an urge I was easily able to ignore.

We drove for about twenty minutes before entering an area definitely seedier than the area where we'd spent the last few hours. I actually felt way more at home in this area, as it was closer to what I was used to—decrepit. The buildings were more rundown, there were bars on the windows of the stores to prevent break-ins, and the people milling around the sidewalks were dressed in worn clothes. There was no sign of the glitz and glam here.

I looked down at my dress and frowned. "What are we doing?" I finally asked as we pulled up next to a non-descript warehouse building.

Hendrix's face was perfectly blank, and a chill filled me. It was like he'd closed off all of his emotions.

"Hendrix?" I asked softly.

"It's crucial to my business that there's never an appearance of weakness. What's about to happen is imperative for not only my business but also the livelihood of all the people I support and employ. Can you understand that?"

I frowned. "Um, I suppose so, but that doesn't answer my question."

"You'll see," he said grimly, his face still not showing any emotion.

I bit my lip but didn't say anything else. Hendrix's driver opened his door, and Hendrix slid out. I followed awkwardly behind, not used to wearing such a long, tight dress. The other man was standing by Hendrix when I finally got out of the car, and I watched as he handed Hendrix something in a brown paper bag.

Fear and foreboding were quickly filling up my insides. "Maybe I could just stay in the car?" I offered, but none of the men seemed amused or willing to take me up on my offer.

"Let's go," Hendrix ordered without answering me. "Stay by her," he growled at the other man. He must have trusted him more than the driver because he didn't even blink as he came up next to me and firmly grasped my elbow.

"Can you at least tell me your name?" I hissed, annoyance quickly overcoming my fear as he yanked me forward after Hendrix.

I was going to have whiplash after this. Who knew that the same man currently striding forward in front of me was the same man who'd been practically offering me the world just a little bit earlier.

Even my wolf wasn't happy right now, and Hendrix had seemed unable to do any wrong to her.

"If he wanted you to know my name, he would have said," the guy grunted, and I shot him a poisonous glare that literally had no effect on him.

Hendrix led us along the side of the warehouse, and I frowned when I heard what sounded like music pulsing from within.

What was this place?

I got my answer when we rounded the corner in the back and I saw that there was a long line of people waiting to get through a pair of double doors roped off with a black velvet rope, music streaming out of the doorway.

Was this some kind of club?

Two giant men were standing by the velvet rope, and it was almost comical to see them literally jump out of their skins when they saw Hendrix approaching. One of them sprouted hair all over his face, and I watched in interest as it sprouted and retracted a few times while he tried to get himself under control. The other one began to grow a snout, long teeth filling up his smile.

Before he could fully shift, Hendrix was in front of him, his terrifying claws extended on just his right hand. He reached out and, without pause, sliced across the man's neck, a splash of red blood rushing out all over the front of Hendrix's previously pristine white dress shirt. A second later, he was slicing across the abdomen of the other bouncer, the man's intestines falling out onto the ground in front of them, steam rising from his innards in the cool night.

A scream erupted from my throat, followed by bile at the bloody sight, and the asshole next to me gripped my arm tighter like I'd suddenly become a flight risk.

Hendrix's driver handed him a handkerchief as the people in line all scattered and ran, sobs of terror filling the air. Hendrix wiped his hands off calmly and cracked his neck. "The cameras are off, Mateo?" he asked the guy holding me.

"Yes, boss," *Mateo* responded. I guess I knew his name now since he was the only thing preventing me from falling to the ground in shock. Hendrix didn't look over at me as he nodded in satisfaction.

"Let's go," he told us before he stepped over the dead corpses and sauntered through the doorway that led inside the warehouse.

Mateo began to walk forward, dragging me along, and I cried out when my foot slipped in the blood seeping from one of the bodies.

"Get ahold of yourself," he muttered to me in disgust, like I was offending him. "You're going to need to have a stronger stomach to live in this world."

"I never asked for this world," I choked out, and then I threw up my dinner all over the front of him.

"Fuck," Mateo growled as he let go of me and stared at the front of his shirt in shock.

"What's the holdup?" Hendrix snapped, popping his head back out of the doorway and staring at us. He looked at the vomit covering the entire front of his guy but didn't say anything about it.

"Coming," Mateo said through gritted teeth before grabbing my arm again and dragging me towards the doorway.

I let him yank me forward, my body descending into shock in the face of all that had happened.

The music grew louder as we went through the entrance. Hendrix was obviously very familiar with the building. He went through door after door decisively until we stepped through a one and found ourselves standing on a balcony that overlooked a dance floor filled with hundreds of people writhing and dancing against each other. I'd never been to a dance club, and my eyes took in the black walls and red tables lining the outside of the dance floor. Red lights were blinking on and off, giving the whole club an eerie, otherworldly feel... or maybe a hellish feel was the right way to describe it. Since I already knew that Hendrix had a thing for red and black, it didn't stretch the imagination to think that Hendrix owned this bar. But why, then, had he killed those bouncers if they were his employees?

There was a large black bar setup stretching the entire left side of the room, and red-tinted shelves were stacked up against a mirrored wall right behind it. At least ten bartenders were rushing along the bar filling people's orders. Dread curled in my stomach as I looked down at the masses of people, and then back to where Hendrix was staring down at all of them, an unfathomable look in his eyes.

Was he going to...?

Hendrix abruptly turned left and walked along the length of the balcony to where there was another pair of doors. He disappeared inside, followed behind closely by his driver, and then Mateo and me.

We walked down another long hallway until the music behind us had faded and I could hear different music coming from somewhere up ahead.

The music grew louder as we approached a set of red filagree double doors directly ahead of us.

Mateo pulled me slightly behind him, making sure to still keep a tight grip on my arm as he did so. We stopped in front of the double doors and a growl ripped from Hendrix's throat that had goosebumps springing up all over my skin. He pulled a revolver from the brown paper bag that his driver had given him and handed it to the driver.

"I won't be needing that. I've decided this needs to be a bit more...personal," Hendrix spit, and the driver gulped and nodded, gripping the gun tightly in his own hand.

Hendrix nodded at Mateo, and just for a second, his gaze finally flicked towards mine. There was something in his gaze, something that looked faintly like regret before he blinked, and anything I'd seen was replaced by steely-eyed determination.

Hendrix turned back around, took a deep breath, and then lifted his shoe and kicked out at the door, shattering the frame and sending pieces of the door flying. He burst into the room, and for a moment...there was only silence as everyone stared in shock at Hendrix standing in the doorway. I peered into the room and saw what looked like mountains of white powder on a table in the center of the enormous room-- presumably cocaine--scantily clad women with dead eyes draped all over men sitting around other tables, and literally a stack of rifles in the back of the room.

This wasn't good.

"I can explain," a voice finally called out, breaking the silence. Apparently, that had been what Hendrix was waiting for because he leaped forward and transformed into...

A beast.

That was the only way to describe the hulking monster with red eyes standing where Hendrix was moments ago.

The monster was at least ten feet tall, sharp spikes going down the back of his black fur. I couldn't see his face, but I could see the long claws extending out of his paws, claws that I'd had glimpses of before. The beast turned his head to look back at us, and I gasped as I stared into his red, glowing eyes. Serrated teeth that were more like a shark's than a wolf's filled his long snout. His chest heaved as the monster locked eyes with me, and I struggled not to scream as I stared back.

Time stood still for a long moment...and then it was chaos.

Screams filled the room as Hendrix's monster turned back around and leaped at the nearest man in front of him. There was a loud ripping sound, and I jumped as the man's head was suddenly thrown to the ground. It was like a red haze spread across the room as Hendrix tore through at least fifty people that had been in there, blood, guts, and body parts flying everywhere.

I closed my eyes and pressed my face against Mateo's back to block out all the carnage, but what I'd seen felt engraved in my eyelids because the scenes replayed in my head continuously, even as I heard the screams. Mateo's body was trembling slightly, and I could smell the fear emanating from both him and the driver. There was a particularly loud scream, and my eyes flew open as I realized that Mateo had let me go.

I didn't think, I just pushed away from him and took off down the hallway we'd just come from.

"Finish them," I thought I heard Hendrix's voice order, but I didn't look back. I just tore away as fast as I could.

I made it through the doors that led out into the balcony overlooking the dance floor and then hustled down the stairs towards the main level, not really knowing where I was going, but just trying to get far away from what I'd just witnessed.

People gasped as they saw me, and I knew I looked a sight. Blood was all over me from the massacre that I'd just witnessed. Screams sounded out a few seconds later from behind me, and I knew someone was following me. I was inches away from the door on the other side of the floor when a hand grabbed my arm and yanked me backward. I turned and saw a grim-looking Hendrix, and I lost it, pulling and shrieking, clawing at whatever I could reach with my fingernails.

I might as well have been tickling him with feathers for all the emotion he showed as I tore at his neck.

"Bad girl," he growled before scooping me up and walking towards the doors I'd been trying to escape out of. Desperately, I knocked my head forward into his face, a loud crack sounding as I broke his nose. Hendrix sighed as blood began to fall down his face, mixing in with all the other blood that was covering him, and then he turned and tossed me right into the arms of a pissed-off-looking Mateo. I struggled in Mateo's arms as well, but it was hopeless. I watched as Hendrix manually snapped his nose back into place until it was perfect once again and wiped at his face with a cloth that his driver had handed him.

I looked over Mateo's shoulder only to see everyone dancing again, blissfully unaware of what had happened upstairs and not caring about the girl that was being carted off against her will.

I was taken down one more hallway before we passed through an exit that led outside. I gulped down the cool air that felt like nirvana compared to the humid, hot, sweat-filled air we'd just come from around the dance floor.

Taking a deep breath for good measure, I reared back and kneed Mateo in the junk, causing him to immediately drop me. I scrambled to my feet and took off.

I'd only made it a few steps before I was grabbed by Hendrix once again.

"Please let me go," I whimpered.

"Never," Hendrix whispered fiercely, the growl of his monster wolf threaded in his voice.

I'd been kidnapped by a monster.

There was a sudden sharp stab in my neck, and then everything mercifully went black.

A warm, humid wind and a soft mist of water brushing against my face was the first thing I became aware of. My eyelids felt like they'd been glued shut as I struggled to come back into full consciousness.

My body bounced up and down, and I finally succeeded in opening my eyes only to wish I was still asleep. I was laying on a leather couch in nothing but a long shirt that had to be Hendrix's, judging by the fact it was coated in his scent. I struggled to sit up, the massive headache I'd experienced the last time Hendrix had knocked me out, beating through my head.

Hopefully there weren't long-term effects from being constantly drugged. Although, did it really matter? With what I'd seen at the club, it was only a matter of time before he killed me too.

Monsters didn't have exceptions.

There was a large open window behind me, and I could see nothing but water as far as the eye could see. In any other circumstance, I would have been enthralled, but my rose-colored glasses had been ripped off and all the magic of my new world was gone.

The boat must have hit a rough wave because my stomach fell out from under me as it moved up and down in a rocking motion I hadn't experienced before and wasn't a fan of. I needed to get out of here before I threw up, not that there was much in my stomach to throw up.

I looked around the tiny room for a pair of shorts or something to put on even though the shirt went all the way to my knees. I sighed in relief when I spotted a pair of shorts folded neatly by the narrow door.

I reached for the knob, fully expecting for it to be locked, and to my surprise, it clicked open with ease. I tentatively pushed open the door to see a large open area filled with several comfy-looking couches. Several girls were lounging on the couches watching a huge tv playing a chick flick that I remembered. Looking closer at the girls, I realized that I recognized them. They were all fully dressed now, their makeup scrubbed clean of their faces. But there was no denying it. It was the girls I'd glimpsed in the room right before Hendrix had painted it red.

I'd thought he'd killed them.

There were five of them in total, and they all stared at me, various looks of uncertainty on their faces. A few of them smiled, but they all remained quiet.

"Hello," I finally said.

"Hi," the one seated closest to me answered shyly, her Russian accent thick. Unlike how out of it her eyes had been while in that room, they were clear now, if exhausted looking.

"You're from the club," I said, my head spinning in confusion.

The girl's gaze darkened. "We'd been sold to those men." She spit in disgust.

They'd been victims of sex trafficking, I realized, sorrow coursing through me. Hendrix had...saved them then?

Something that felt a little bit like hope flickered through me. Until a dark thought hit me.

Had he just spared them so that he could use them on his islands?

They might be even worse off.

Except for some reason, the idea didn't ring true in my obviously stupid heart.

"I'm glad you're okay," I finally whispered hoarsely, rubbing at my aching forehead and not knowing what else to say.

The girls nodded, looking haunted, and I made my way past them to the door on the other side of the room that I could tell led out to the deck. The rocking motion of the boat was still making me sick, and I figured getting some fresh air might help.

I spotted Hendrix immediately. He was leaning over the railing staring out ahead of him. I hadn't been able to see anything from the room, but out here I could see a large island straight ahead of us. There were tall, sand-colored stone walls all around the perimeter...and palm trees.

A paradisiacal prison.

Hendrix looked back over his shoulder and lifted an eyebrow, silently daring me to approach him.

As soon as I saw him though, I was assaulted by images of him tearing those people apart.

Even knowing they were bad men...it had been shocking. Macabre images to join in with the ones I already had from my family's demise on that fateful night.

Mateo was a few feet away talking to a group of men I hadn't yet seen, freshly cleaned, as was Hendrix. He looked at me warily, probably afraid that I was going to throw up on him again, or worse, hit him in the balls.

I didn't feel bad at all.

I went to the other side of the boat, away from all of them, and took deep breaths, trying to calm down my nausea and headache.

I would have asked for one of those little magic pills Hendrix had given me at the start of this whole journey...but that would have required me actually talking to him. And I wasn't quite ready for that.

I watched as the island got closer and closer until I could see the colorful buildings built up behind the imposing wall, and the people working on the shore with various nets and what looked like fishing poles. I could feel Hendrix's gaze on me almost the whole time, practically begging for me to look at him. But I could be very stubborn, obviously, and never took the bait.

Our boat, a sleek black and red vessel that was probably closer to a yacht than a boat, pulled up next to the dock that stretched out at least a hundred feet from the shoreline.

We were here.

"Ready to see your new life?" asked Hendrix, making me jump since I'd somehow missed him approaching me.

"Hardly," I responded sarcastically, and he chuckled like I was nothing more than an ornery little kitten instead of a furious woman who'd witnessed him slaughter a room full of people.

My wolf sniffed indignantly, obviously not happy with him either. It was a relief that she'd gotten the memo. I hated being at odds with her, and she'd been all too quiet in the club.

Four men were waiting at the end of the dock, and they worked quickly with some of the men on board to secure the ship. Just a few minutes later, a door was unlatched, revealing a wide plank that had been connected to the ship's side.

Hendrix firmly grasped my arm and began to lead me down the plank onto the dock. Some of the workers eyed me curiously, but they quickly averted their gazes when Hendrix's menacing growl made an appearance.

Oh, so he was back to the possessive asshole routine.

Good to know.

The walk down the dock was long, but there was so much to see that we were on the shore before I knew it.

I was barefoot since the heels I'd been wearing had disappeared and no one had offered me anything to wear. As soon as I stepped onto the sand beyond the dock, I stopped, wigging my toes at the sensation of the sand brushing against my skin.

I enjoyed the feel of the sand for a long minute, belatedly realizing that Hendrix wasn't yanking me away. I looked over to see what he was doing and saw that he was just standing next to me, looking at me with a softness in his gaze that I was determined to ignore.

Maybe there had been a good reason for what happened in that room, but I wasn't quite at the stage where a brutal massacre was the answer. There were probably people in the world that could have come up with reasons to support my father's actions as well.

"Ready when you are," I said to Hendrix, trying to ignore the fear and uncertainty I was experiencing as I took my attention away from the palm trees and golden sand and faced the compound in front of me.

And it really was a compound. Now that we were close, I could see a guard station set up, and men dressed in white tank tops and military-grade pants with huge AK-47s. They were everywhere, and obviously ready for an attack.

There was a thick metal gate in the wall, and I watched as it retracted, revealing a neatly paved cobblestone street bordered by sandstone-colored houses. People were milling around in the streets, most of them soldiers, and just beyond the row of houses I could see a glimpse of what looked like an enormous courtyard area with people doing various training exercises judging by the faint sound of someone barking orders.

The soldiers we passed gave respectful nods to Hendrix,

but no one stopped to talk to us, which apparently was what Hendrix wanted because he moved us swiftly down the street and into the courtyard. Once in the courtyard, I could see military-style barracks in the distance, but they only caught my attention for a second because of the enormous mansion rising up in front of us.

"Welcome to Isla de Sangre," Hendrix murmured as he yanked me across the giant courtyard and through an archway that revealed a gorgeous Olympic-style pool...

And a group of soldiers watching two naked girls making out.

I quickly averted my eyes, only to see a gorgeous man lounging on a pool chair...getting a blowjob.

What the fuck?

CASPIAN

Getting a blowjob wasn't always the answer, but it sure as fuck helped.

I lounged in the sun chair by the glistening pool, my legs spread, and a cute brunette kneeling between them like she worshiped me. Maybe she did, especially as her rosy mouth slid down over my cock, taking me deeper.

I groaned, trying to focus on her soft lips, her wicked tongue, and my tip hitting the back of her throat as she accommodated all of me into her mouth.

Her eyes glazed over, lost in her own ecstasy.

Females were simply a means to an end... a glorious end indeed, and just like all the others who entertained me, they helped me forget things. Escape from the past, from nightmares, from what I had to do this morning after I was left alone to fix a treacherous problem. After the shit storm of discovering more than one man was involved in stealing arms from us and eliminating them, well, I'd deserved some R&R time.

My cock popped out of the brunette's mouth, and she blinked at me, drawing my attention to her. What was her name... Started with an S, I'm sure. Sara, that was it. She looked ready to ask me a question.

"What can I do for you, pet?" I asked.

"Figured we could move into your room and take this further." She batted her eyes, licking her lips. She wore only the tiniest string bikini bottom, and her small breasts were perky, nipples tight and beaded, just begging for my mouth.

I knew why she asked, and it had nothing to do with being shy. For one, we were in the outdoor pool area of our mansion, the Khan pack compound. Guards were lined across the ten-foot stone wall surrounding our property. Others lingered in the shadows nearby, guns at the ready. Not to mention, there were three women splashing naked in the pool. All of them were watching us constantly.

But Sara wanted me to fuck her where all my attention would be focused on her.

Except, it wasn't what I was in the mood for.

I noticed her glancing at my lap, and I looked down to the streak of dried blood across my forearm. Fear crowded behind her eyes. I must have missed a spot in cleaning up after this morning's fiasco. Everyone who worked here knew who we were and what we did. And that pissing us off was a mistake they'd never forget.

"O-only i-if you're interested, of course," she whispered, half-stuttering.

"You know what I want," I stated, reclining my head back on the chair, the earlier tension from having killed three men stretching over my mind. Fuck. This was my time out to forget all that shit, but now they were all I thought about.

"They're over there," Jay, my second in command, growled, his breath heavy from us running across the whole damn island like madmen.

Trees crowded around us, throwing shadows over everything, but up ahead, the sunlight beamed between the trunks like a beacon. Beyond the woods, three pack members were on the pebbled beach. They hurriedly packed a large speed boat with wooden boxes. Based on the missing cargo from our storage room, I knew they were filled with guns and ammo.

Everyone at the compound knew their place because crossing my brothers and me came with devastating results.

My wolf snarled with fury in my chest, rage biting into me, as did my transformation. There was no denying it. I hadn't wanted to believe it when Jay first told me he spotted the men sneaking into the woods with our merchandise. But now that I witnessed Lun, the man I'd known for five years and shared drinks with on many occasions, stealing from me first hand, my insides turned livid.

The idiot was me for trusting Lun, for telling him things I never should have revealed. But I guessed now his words of loyalty meant fuck all when his actions screamed the truth.

My clothes shredded off me, and I charged out of the woods in my wolf form, dark fur ruffled in the breeze. I unleashed a horrendous howl, and they all jerked in my direction with terror in their eyes.

And they needed to be scared.

I lunged, my teeth bared.

None of them would survive the day.

"You still want me, right, Caspian?" Sara asked softly, lifting her gaze, batting those fake, long lashes. Her voice lulled me out of my thoughts, and my attention fell to her plump lips.

She kissed me along the seam of my knee where the bottom half was a synthetic leg after a horrendous attack years ago.

My frustration flared, and I pushed her away from my leg. Did I mention I'd had a shit day?

"Are you currently sucking on my cock?" I snarled.

A long pause of silence stretched out between us as it took her a few moments to understand my question.

Then she blanched, blinking at me. "Of course." She rapidly curled her fingers around my shaft, her tongue tasting me. I drew in a sharp breath as she pushed the entire length into her slick mouth.

I moaned and let myself sink into the sensation once more as she worked her lips over my erection. Anticipation of coming buzzed through me as I craved that high that stole me away from this world, even if for a few moments.

Now, where were we?

Thoughts dissolved as her hand wrapped around my balls. She drew me in and out with practiced moves, and I hissed each time I hit the curve of her throat. Sara was known for her cock-sucking abilities, and it was one of the reasons we kept her around. We all had our specialties, and there was no shame in it.

"That's it, open up, take it all," I insisted, tilting my hips up to bump that spot in her throat again and again.

Loud footsteps echoed from my right, and I roared from the intrusion. I glanced to my right with a sneer.

Hendrix marched across the cobblestone path stretching from the gate to the grand entrance of our home. And he held the hand of a woman by his side, dragging her with him. She was a petite thing, dark red and purple hair, wearing casual clothes. She didn't look like someone who belonged here.

They were about ten feet from me, and even with him not looking my way, I could see his usual pissed demeanor... What else was new?

He'd returned from his trip to the Madfur pack, except he'd come back with someone. That hadn't been part of our deal.

He hauled the gorgeous little redhead alongside him, and she stumbled to keep up with his long strides. Her gaze swung up to the enormous sandstone mansion, all three floors and fifteen bedrooms. We had built the house after we purchased the island. After all, we needed privacy for our business, not to mention security, plus a spot to enjoy all our spoils. Added to that, we were close to Reject Island, aiding in our trading business.

"Brother," Hendrix stated, not bothering to glance my way. "We need to talk."

But I couldn't keep my eyes off her.

With the way she'd kept her distance from Hendrix, despite him holding onto her hand tightly, she wasn't enjoying being handled roughly, and I liked watching the way she pulled against him. Her determination was kind of fucking hot. She had a streak of stubbornness, and I could see that being an issue with Hendrix.

When her piercing, emerald eyes rolled up to meet mine, I saw pure animalistic hunger behind them. She watched Sara sucking on my cock, and the redhead's mouth dropped open. I'd be lying if it didn't turn me on. I found myself sniffing the air for her scent, but it was upwind from me.

She tensed, and shadows danced across her face from the swaying palm trees as she struggled to look away.

My cock twitched, and I might have been going cross-eyed from how turned on I was right then, how the sight of her had me positively ready to burst in Sara's mouth. I paused at that moment, the rest of the world fading. She had large, innocent eyes and wore an expression of fear and curiosity across her delicate features.

Fuck me, but she was the most gorgeous creature I'd ever laid eyes on.

My cock hardened to the point it hurt.

Who the hell was she, anyway? How could a person be so captivating... so beautiful? Gasping for breath, all I could think about was taking in her taste to discover if she was as delectable as she looked.

Hendrix yanked her up the steps to the front door, her curvy ass catching my attention, those toned legs, and my thoughts flew to me buried between them. Guys had their favorite female body parts, the things that could always turn them on. For me, it was their pussy. I craved it, wanted to bathe in the scent, and needed the slick all over my face.

But she was making me think I could be an ass man.

My balls tightened with the deepening pressure.

And just as they popped out of sight, and my thoughts shot to me buried deep between those sweet thighs, I lost it. I thrust my hips toward Sara's mouth and held it there as I trembled. My orgasm smacked through my body, and I pulsed into her, flooding her with my seed. She worked her neck, swallowing down everything as I growled savagely.

I collapsed onto my back, having no fucking idea what just happened. My reaction to the redhead was a marvel and something I hadn't felt with another woman in a very long time.

Well, color me fucking surprised.

I pulled out of Sara's mouth, and she kneeled back, wiping her mouth with the back of her hand. Any other day, and after that performance, I might have considered devouring her pussy or fingering her as a reward...I mean, I wasn't a monster. But now, the sight of the new girl left me eager to drag myself inside and find out who she was. My instincts begged me to pull her aside and look into her eyes as I stripped off her clothes. A groan rolled from my wolf at the thought.

"Thanks, Sara," I stated as I got to my feet and grabbed my jeans that were hanging off the back of the seat before climbing into them.

"My name's Katie," Sara said.

Still gasping for breath after my reaction to the newcomer, I nodded absentmindedly and made my way to the front door.

I had to find out who she was. And why the hell Hendrix had brought her here. Everyone who came onto our island served a purpose. Maybe she was our new plaything.

Cold tiles cooled my feet as I paused in the hallway. Before me rose the marble staircase leading up to the second and third floor. I listened for where my brother had gone, wondering if he'd take her to the bedrooms.

A servant in a cream dress and white apron rushed past me, her head low and not looking me in the eyes. Others hurried around the place like ants busying themselves with keeping the mansion running. Cleaning the place, feeding us and the guards, caring for our frequent guests and the pack members who lived on this island. Woodlands spread widely behind the mansion, housing close to fifty wolf shifters on top of our men. This place was our paradise.

I walked toward the stairs, then changed my mind. With the way Hendrix was hauling the girl around, he might be tossing her into one of the prison cells we'd built in the basement.

My mind kept conjuring up images of her... that tight little body with those perfect curves calling to any man to take a bite out of her. Seductive lips, juicy tits, and eyes screaming vulnerability. She had that look that drew me to her and made me want to wrap her up in cotton wool.

What the fuck was my brother doing by bringing someone like that into our home?

Just as I started to move toward the basement, I caught Hendrix coming down the steps, alone. He'd put her up in a bedroom after all. Was she *his* new sex toy? We always shared the girls... And that left me curious to know exactly if she was available.

I turned to him, and I followed him into the parlor room, a place where we often entertained business partners. The walls were covered in bookshelves, and there were three leather couches in a U-shape in the middle, surrounding a coffee table. It was a porcelain statue of a naked woman on her hands and knees, the glass top balanced on her back.

Hendrix took a seat in the center of a sofa, reclining, his legs wide and arms stretched out across the back. It wasn't uncommon to find him twisting deals in a dozen ways in this room to get what he wanted, but he'd never come home with a woman before as part of his paying someone a lesson.

"Who is she?" I asked and sat my ass on the arm of the couch.

"Emersyn was a deal I struck with the Madfur pack leader."

"Deal?" I eyed him carefully, knowing every step Hendrix took was calculated and on purpose. "When you say deal, you mean you killed Brayden, right?"

His lips thinned with that threatening look as his eyes darkened. But, if there was anyone who would stand up to Hendrix, it was me and our brother River. And I wasn't backing down about this. We ruled this pack and our territories with an iron fist, and that meant not letting emotions get in the way.

He leaned forward, eyes narrowing. "She's a reward I couldn't walk away from. Plus, she was important to Brayden."

My muscles automatically tensed. "So, that fucking prick still lives?" Like my brothers, we punished anyone who crossed us, and Hendrix possessed an uncanny ability to scare the shit out of anyone. He always got his way, so what the fuck changed that?

The girl came to mind. She'd crawled under his skin and gotten to him.

Hendrix shrugged. "Back the fuck off, Caspian. I made the terms, and I took her as payment, along with the money owed. If you have a problem with that, then keep your distance from her."

I reared my shoulders back, not remembering the last time my brother had been this defensive of anyone except us... his family.

She had definitely done something to him... and from my reaction outside, she'd done something to me, too.

"She's different," he muttered, a slight smile touching his lips like his thoughts were on the girl as he spoke about her.

"I can see that. Just so long as you don't end up as her puppet on strings. Like Father used to say, never assume that someone being quiet and meek is a sign of weakness."

He barked a laugh. "Since when have you become the man of reason?"

I grinned. "Since I'm always covering your ass and River's. Speaking of which, River's gonna flip. You know he doesn't trust newcomers."

His brows furrowed. "He'll have to deal with it," Hendrix snapped. "She's staying. End of discussion. Everything goes on as normal. No distractions."

I raised my hands in a show of defense. "You don't need to convince me. I'm never one to say no to another sweet ass and tits around the place."

My mind wouldn't shut off from picturing Emersyn, from the shock on her face as she watched me getting a blow job. The edge she awakened in me intrigued me more than I expected, so I understood why Hendrix had become so captivated by her as well.

"Any news from River?" I asked, trying to distract myself from my thoughts. I was getting hard again, and I didn't want Hendrix to smell my lust. He didn't need to know I wanted to bang the new girl...at least not yet.

Hendrix shook his head. "Scouting mission shouldn't take too long. He's due home soon. What about around here?

What did I miss while I was gone?" he asked, studying a maid as she rushed past our room.

"Shovelling shit basically. I found out where our missing cargo's been going... it was more than one man, as we initially thought, stealing from us. Jay tracked down Lun and two others from the pack trying to escape the island with boxes of our guns."

He stiffened, his brow furrowing. "Fucking sonofabitch! Where are they?"

"Six feet under."

His pinched brow deepened. "Okay, so we might have more infiltrators in our team. I want a complete sweep, and everything gets searched. Rooms, homes, pockets. I don't give a fuck!" He barked the words, those freaky claws of his extending and retracting as he tried to get himself under control.

"Already on it. I've got Jay coordinating a thorough search."

Hendrix jolted to his feet, sneering. "Goddamn cocksuckers." He shoved the longer strands of hair out of his face and marched out of the room.

"Where are you off to?"

But he didn't respond. Instead, he turned down the hallway toward the rear of the mansion. Of course he was pissed, and his shakedown would rattle the entire island.

My gaze shifted to the stairs, and I wondered what room Hendrix had put her in.

I climbed up directly to the third floor, where all our bedrooms were, curious to find out more. It wasn't often that a stranger made such an impact on us, and I wanted to understand who we were dealing with.

Sniffing the air, her faint scent found me... sugary sweet with a hint of clementine, and something else I couldn't quite pick... almost metallic. I followed it, surprised to find myself strolling right past Hendrix's room.

In moments, I stood outside one of the spare bedrooms we mostly used for storing crap. Excitement zapped up my spine, and my mind flooded with images of me down by the pool as she arrived, of how much I hadn't been able to get her out of my thoughts since.

I reached for the handle and found it locked. Of course he'd keep her imprisoned, which told me she wasn't necessarily in agreement with this decision to come here.

Stretching an arm to the top frame over the door, I patted the dust until my fingers grazed the metal key.

Giving a small knock and not receiving a response, I jammed the key in, unlocked it, and opened the door slowly.

"Hope you've got clothes on, but even if you don't, I'm entering."

CASPIAN

Bright light drenched the bedroom. A breeze fluttered into the room through the open balcony doors, throwing the curtains into a billowing wave. The bathroom door stood open too.

But my sights landed on the red-haired woman... She had her back to me, halfway through tugging a shirt down her head, her back and thin waist exposed. She was so petite, and I spied the wounds on her back.

Burn marks covered her milky white skin, and unease tightened in my gut. What the fuck had happened to her?

Hurriedly covering herself, she jerked around, her eyebrows pulled together with clear anger. She studied me, her gaze zipping up and down my body. But I didn't miss the embarrassment on her blushing cheeks.

"I'm not going to suck your cock, if that's what you're thinking," she snapped.

Moon Goddess, have mercy on me.

I couldn't help myself as I burst out laughing. "Don't worry, that's not my intention, although it's always welcome. I just came to inspect the girl who caught my brother's attention and made him break his cardinal rule of not stealing women. I'm Caspian, by the way. Hendrix is my brother."

She blinked at me, seeming lost.

I was feeling a little lost too. I couldn't get the images of her scars out of my head. It tightened my heart, and my wolf whined at me. He unleashed a low growl in my chest at the thought of any harm coming to her. I considered grabbing her into my arms possessively, to brush away her fears, to find out who hurt her so I could kill them in the most horrendous way possible. Something about her made me desperate to protect her... and I'd never felt this way about any other woman.

It seemed my wolf was in protective mode over this delicate creature. That was new.

The more I kept picturing her injuries, the more my memories sank into their own battle. As if on cue, a lacerating, burning pain whipped across my left knee, and I winced on the inside.

I'd lost the bottom half of my leg in a brutal pack fight, and the agony still lingered all these years later.

They called it phantom limb syndrome, but whenever I thought about the past, I swore I still felt my toes and that I could wriggle them. The pain that shouldn't exist, returned.

I had a synthetic half-leg that could easily be mistaken for a real leg by anyone looking. It was amazing what money could buy... but no surgery in the world could eradicate the memories staining my thoughts.

The chaotic battle flashed in my mind like images in a movie reel.

Bloody massacres.

Screams and people running in every direction.

So many gruesome bodies.

The stench of smoke from homes burning, choking on the stench.

And me ending up cornered by our rivals...

My stomach trembled and then hardened as I shoved the thoughts aside.

I hated reliving them, hated remembering how our enemy had attacked in the dead of night, hated being overpowered. I might have been only fourteen when it happened, but it didn't seem to make a difference to the pain that never left me. I accepted long ago that I would live with this hurt for life. Not that it made it easier.

I shook off the sensation rattling me and found the stunning girl watching me curiously...and concerned. My breath was coming out in gasps, and a drop of perspiration rolled down my spine.

"Are you okay?" she asked softly.

For a moment, I had to consider her question, my head still trapped in the past. I frowned, mentally pushing the images away, but I couldn't stop the screams in my ears, the pain of losing half my leg to an axe. It vibrated through every inch of my being, and even my wolf winced.

The problem with surviving such a wound was that it left you broken. A growl keened from my throat, but I'd taught myself to not let that depressing shit consume me ever again. After the attack, I'd fallen into a hole I never thought I'd escape from. But Hendrix and River saved me; they were by my side every day, so failing and returning to that wasn't an option.

I straightened myself, clearing the haze from my eyes, hating to show weakness, and feeling uneasy that it had happened in front of our new guest.

She stood in front of me, watching with soft eyes, and she had her hand stretched out to touch me, to check on me. That small gesture of affection made me realize just how special she was. In this world, strangers didn't care about others...

Her touch quickly moved past giving me comfort though,

rousing thoughts of what I wanted to do to her, how I wanted to run my tongue over her body.

She quickly pulled back and wrapped her arms around her middle like she couldn't believe she'd just touched me.

"Emersyn—" I began.

"Call me Syn," she corrected me in a velvety smooth voice. "I don't mind if you call me that."

Tension melted from my body at the sweetness of her voice. The earnest feelings behind her words brought me more comfort than she'd ever know.

To be honest with myself, her reaction surprised me. Maybe my wolf was onto something when he grew protective of her instantly.

She hastily unraveled her arms and patted down her deep blue shirt, staring past the open French doors leading to the balcony. "The view up here is ridiculous."

I licked my lips as she stepped outside, and I followed, pushing the fluttering curtains aside as I watched the sway of her hips. I stayed closer to her back, the breeze throwing locks of her hair into my face. Silky soft, her hair smelled like flowers, and my fingers twitched at the need to take her, my cock pulsing.

She stretched on the large balcony, arms in the air, her shirt riding up, revealing her midriff.

Standing that close to her, she was even more beautiful than I initially thought. The sun blinked against her riveting green eyes, her full lips partially open as she drew in a shuddered breath while taking in the stunning sights from up here.

"It's breathtaking from up here," she murmured.

"It sure is," I said, staring at her rather than the sprawling mansion grounds. I knew it like the back of my hand... the pool down below, palm trees lining white beaches, and even the outdoor dining terrace. Woodland spread out on either side of us, and over the tops of the lofty walls, our yachts bobbed in the crystal blue water of the shoreline. Not a cloud in the sky, nothing but paradise.

I kept my attention on Syn though, this incredibly gorgeous woman. With it came a desperate hunger, consuming me, and a craving to move closer to her with every fiber of my being. She was a beautiful distraction, and an unbearable need shot straight to my dick. I'd never had my body react so instantaneously. It was partly unnerving, partly arousing.

She chewed on her lower lip, tilting her head back, eyes closing as she took in the sun.

Part of me worried how quickly I found myself drawn to her. How the temptation to wrench her against me and bend her over as I fucked her pussy burned through my skull.

She opened her eyes and gave me a sharp stare. "So, what does one do here, aside from…" She glanced down to the pool and back at me, not finishing her sentence.

"Anything we want," I responded easily. "When my brothers and I bought this island, we did so with the intention of no one ever telling us what to do again."

Her pink lips twisted in anguish, which confused me at first. "Except for the slaves who work for you. They have no such freedom." She turned her attention back to the splendor of the landscape.

"There are no slaves here. Everyone receives a fair salary for their services."

"What does that make me then? I'm locked up, aren't I?"

"It's for your own safety," I insisted, convinced that had to be the reason Hendrix kept her locked up. I didn't want to mention that there was a chance he wanted to keep her as his own personal sex toy.

With that thought alone, a possessiveness rose through me, and instinct begged me to draw her closer to me, to rip off her shirt and bite down on that creamy skin. I wanted to mark her so that everyone would know she belonged to me.

Except, I knew my brother. He was feeling something for her, I could see that just by talking to him. This girl was going to be a problem. I could tell already. Was she even aware of the effect she had on us?

My hands were shaking from the effort of not reaching out to touch her and see if her skin was as soft as it looked. A hitched breath came out of her as she looked at the shoreline, and she looked so fucking fragile at that moment. So innocent...

I couldn't help but think that despite my intense attraction to Syn, I had done some really fucked up shit, as had my brothers. Was it a smart move to bring someone so innocent into our lives? There was a reason we had guards with guns across the entire island. We had enemies who wanted us all dead, and I doubted she fully realized what she'd walked into.

"Keep me safe from what?" she asked.

I pulled my lips into a reassuring smile. "It's an island. There are all sorts of wild beasts in the woods who wouldn't hesitate to attack someone as beautiful as you," I told her, intentionally vague about the fact that the 'wild beasts' weren't exactly animals.

She swallowed loudly and didn't respond right away. "I don't want to be stuck in a cage," she whispered, her hand coming up to her throat. "I might as well be sent back to the Madfur pack then." Disdain filled her voice as though it took a lot of effort to admit something like that.

I let out a sigh. "Believe it or not, you could have a good life here. When you leave the room, it just has to be with us or escorted by someone."

I was making things up on the spot right now, obviously having no idea what Hendrix had planned. But I was on board with any plan that prevented her from running away. And I could tell right now she was definitely a flight risk.

I closed the distance between us with one long step, and my shadow played across her face. She recoiled, her back hitting the stone railing from the balcony. I wasn't sure she believed me, but my word was something she'd have to learn to accept.

No one wanted to be imprisoned, but I could tell right now that my wolf had no intention of letting her get away.

She caught me studying her, and something glinted in the sunlight on her wrists. Bronze bands that looked more like shackles than jewelry pieces. I took her hand in mine, expecting her to yank it away, but she didn't resist. Her skin was silky smooth and soft, and all I could think was how careful I had to be with her.

"What's this?" I asked, looking at the bracelet and noting that she also had an identical one on her other wrist.

She licked her lips nervously. "A little something to remind me of my place from my fated mate in the Madfur pack. It suppresses my wolf so I can't get away from him."

I watched intently as an array of emotions flared across her delicate face, from embarrassment to blinking tears from her eyes, and finally coming to a resolute tightness of her expression. Hot, white rage rushed through me as "fated mate" absorbed into my brain.

"Your fated mate did this to you?" Hendrix's words came back to me about Syn being someone special to Brayden. He *was* her fated mate... Why else would he keep her wolf locked away? I'd despised the guy before, but now I had a newfound hatred for him, and I was already rummaging through my mind for the cruelest way to torture him.

Hung by his toes, then unleash wasps on him? While painful, it wouldn't give me the satisfaction of getting my hands dirty. No... the bastard deserved something more fitting, a slow death that involved breaking every bone, one at a time, and ensuring he never passed out. Hmm, I'd have to work on it; I knew I could do better.

Syn raised an eyebrow, watching me cautiously.

Nothing could encapsulate the primal fury tearing across my body of what he'd done to her. To have her wolf suppressed was like ripping out her soul and leaving her with half a life. And was he responsible for the burns on her back too?

For now, I would tend to her while she stayed with us, but one thing I knew with certainty was that she would never return to the Madfur pack. I would make sure of that. I would obliterate Brayden and his father, Anton, before I let them touch her ever again. Fated mate or not.

I went to finger the band on her wrist when she flinched her hand back.

"Don't. If you try to take it off, it'll zap you."

"What does it do to you?"

She hesitated at first, and an expression filled with pain flared over her face. "The same if I try to take it off." Those beautiful lips tugged downward, and my destructive tendencies floated forward once more.

Fury scorched across my chest, knowing that Hendrix hadn't murdered Brayden.

As much as I didn't want her in the firing range of the dangers that came with our life, the more I stared at the band, the more my blood boiled. Her fated mate put her in harm's way on purpose. His heinous act infuriated me.

Maybe I'd underestimated Hendrix as to why he brought Syn into our home.

"Hendrix said he's going to bring a witch to remove the bands," she explained, almost hopeful.

"That's a good idea," I murmured. "We'll get that off you

soon. And I'll make you a promise that I will personally murder your fated mate for doing this to you."

Silence danced between us. "I've never had anyone stand up for me before, but I don't want you and your brother to endanger yourself for me."

Fuck, she was sweet.

"My brothers and I are the things nightmares are made of. We'll bring war to their doors and burn down their worlds for crossing us. You don't have to worry about us."

Her mouth gaped open as she stared at me in shock. I was shocking myself as well at the moment.

After a long pause where she turned toward the ocean front views, she said, "You know what's funny?"

"What's that?"

"It's ironic how you act all concerned about this bracelet, but don't bat an eye that I'm held prisoner in this room. But I guess it's okay if you're the one holding me against my will."

Touché. And somehow, she looked even more positively radiant when she was mad. "Okay, then, I guess I have to prove we're different," I countered. "But I want to know. Who gave you the scars on your back? Was it Brayden, because I'll have to figure out a way to kill him twice if it was." A low growl rolled through my chest, and her gaze widened at the deep sound.

She stiffened, not responding but holding my gaze.

Fine, she didn't want to talk about it, but I would find out what happened and take a pound of flesh for every injury on her body from whoever did that to her.

I headed back inside, deciding not to push the point. She would talk when she was ready. "As much as you dislike hearing it, it sounds to me like you're in a better position here than with your fated mate."

"That's still to be proven."

I opened the door to her room and turned toward her. "You coming?"

She didn't answer right away, but looked outside as if expecting something to jump out at her. "Where to?"

"I'll give you a house tour. How does that sound?"

"The entire mansion?" She gasped as if she had never expected such a thing.

"Yep." I omitted the part where I wouldn't show the dungeon or the sex room. If she was well behaved, I might give her a personal tour of it. A place we indulged in our most ultimate fantasies.

I imagined her blushing that lovely scarlet color...all over her body if I took her there... My cock twitched at the image of what I could do to her, how I could show her things she'd never imagined and have her begging for more.

Out in the hallway, she reminded me of a skittish cat. Taking short, quick steps, her head turned in every direction, taking in everything, and part of me wondered if she'd try to make a run for it. Of course, she wouldn't get far. We were on an island, for fuck's sake, but part of me was disappointed she hadn't at least tried to escape. I haven't had myself a good chase for a while. With so many wolves on the island, the small population of rabbits who had once resided here had been eliminated, and there wasn't much else to hunt.

I'd obviously been lying through my teeth about wild beasts in the woods. There was nothing scarier than my brothers and me in this place.

Maybe Hendrix had already instilled enough fear into her to ensure she had limits in her disobedience.

"Is there any chance of getting a drink of water first, please?" She turned to me as we reached the top of the extravagant staircase. She spoke with her sing-song voice, and again it hit me how adorable she was. And I couldn't remember ever thinking of someone being adorable.

"We'll start from the ground floor in the kitchen then, shall we," I offered, mesmerized by her every move. Blood rushed right to my cock as I pictured her naked, her round ass shifting with each step, then grabbing her around her waist and forcing her up against the wall, pinning her in place. The need to touch her was unbearable.

There was something unbelievably intoxicating being around a woman whose every action screamed innocent, yet the confidence in her eyes told me she was a lot more competent than she let on.

Either that, or she was utterly oblivious to the real danger surrounding her.

Down on the ground floor, I led her past the stairs and through several hallways. She walked slowly, completely in awe of the tall ceilings, the crystal chandeliers, expensive paintings in ornate gold frames adorning the walls. Vases and tapestries... Hendrix insisted on only the best and hired a decorator to make this place scream wealth and power. It was for the clients we had visiting... confidence and money closed most deals for us.

She paused in front of a painting, and our arms bumped, me grazing the side of her breast as I stood so close to her. A faint buzz shot through me from the touch, and her hitched breath had me smiling.

"Did you do that on purpose?" she whispered, the corners of her lips tugging upward.

Was she flirting with me?

"Would you like it to be on purpose?" I asked, flashing her a wide smile.

Her grin was authentic, her cheeks coloring, while her gaze dipped from my eyes to my lips. Everything about her was special, and I brushed a loose strand tenderly behind her ear, stepping closer, the heat from her body pouring over me.

"You're perfect," I said.

My wolf stirred, pressing forward. *Mine*, he growled in my mind. *All mine.*

She trembled slightly at my touch.

"You don't need to be shy around me. I can tell you're drawn to me."

"I barely know you," she murmured, lowering her voice, "Even if you are really handsome, it doesn't mean anything. Sometimes the most beautiful things are the deadliest."

"I'll take that as a compliment. And you're incredibly beautiful. I've been thinking about stripping and licking you all over. If you're also deadly, you might just be my perfect match."

Her eyes flickered to the painting and back, her face burning red now. "Tell me about her."

I watched the way she tried to distract me, but I wasn't letting her win. "You're new to this."

With narrowing eyes, she looked my way. "With the painting?"

I chuckled. "With flirting."

She smoothed over her hair with a hand, and her lips pinched to the side. "Oh, is that what we were doing?" she said in a mocking tone.

I liked her a lot. "Your sweet mouth will get you into a lot of trouble."

She laughed softly. "I'll be sure to work on it. Now, are you going to tell me about this painting with the sad woman?"

"Oh, you're genuinely interested?"

She gave me a deadpan expression. "Why else would I stop here? So you can touch my breast?"

With a smile, my mind focused on her perky tits and how much I wanted my cock between them. "You have no clue about all the things I want to touch on you." I struggled to believe just how perfect she was, and how tight my balls were getting with her attempt to flirt with me while being submissive at the same time. She was curious, brazen, and vulnerable.

"And don't pretend you aren't interested," I added.

With a raised eyebrow, she turned away from me to stare at the painting. As much as my hands buzzed to throw her over my shoulder and carry her back into my room to have my way with her, I lowered my gaze to her tight little ass that could easily make any man fall to their knees for her.

It took moments for my senses to come back to reality. Syn was hardly the first woman to have caught my attention, so what was it about her that fascinated me? I had my fun with females, took what I wanted, and walked away. But this girl lingered on my mind, and her scent flooded my nostrils.

I followed her gaze to the portrait of the distraught, naked woman leaning back against a rock. The woman in the painting was covering her face with her arms as though she was crying, her flowing red hair billowing in the wind.

The contrast of the solemn image with that of Syn naked was clashing terribly in my head.

I tried to push those thoughts aside, at least for now, and said, "The name of the piece and artist are unknown, yet it's one of my favorites," I explained, and I looked at the way she studied the portrait, nibbling on her lower lips. She was truly savoring the painting, which I didn't expect. "When I look at it, I see a fallen woman who has reached her lowest point. Her devastation is tragic and beautifully captured."

"She seems to have lost something."

"To me, this painting is inspirational. When she rises again, she will be fierce. Nothing can stop her because when you have nothing to lose, you are untouchable."

Syn twisted her head toward me. "That's very deep, and I like it."

"Me too." Without another word, I placed my hand at her back and guided her right into the kitchen. I was hopeful that once I showed her around, we might end up in one of the many spare bedrooms and I'd show her the real meaning of flirting.

Staff rushed about in the kitchen, washing, collecting supplies from storage, and prepping for tonight's meals.

I moved over to the fridge, opened it, and grabbed a bottle of water, then turned to Syn. Just as I did, Hendrix strolled into the kitchen, and most of the staff made a hasty exit through the rear door.

He only had eyes for Syn though, but when his mouth opened, it wasn't his voice that streamed across the room.

It was River's as he marched in on Hendrix's heels, booming, "Who the fuck is she?"

Syn

Startled, I recoiled until my back hit the kitchen counter, trying my best not to go into complete panic mode.

Caspian swung around, seemingly taken aback by the intrusion, while Hendrix studied me like he was seeing a ghost, or more like he was pissed that I was out of my room. I had no idea not even his brother could escort me to the kitchen.

But the real worry was the new guy who'd burst into the kitchen with us. Alarm bells went off in my mind, and my heartbeat did a stutter. I'd seen men like him back at the Howler Bar, instantly recognizing the type—brash and pushy.

"Shit, River," Caspian barked back. "Want to scare the hell out of her?"

"Do you mean I scared *you*?" He smirked, then turned back to me.

Wild, chestnut hair framed River's strong face, and he didn't even seem to notice Hendrix giving him a death glare. Instead, he watched me, his head tilting to the side. His black tee stretched across his chest and biceps, his designer jeans hanging low on his hips. They had a few dark stains on them, and was it wrong that my first thought went to them being blood?

"What's a pretty little thing like you doing here?" Blue eyes shone as brightly as the sky outside. Sharp cheekbones I'd expect on a statue of an Adonis coupled with the shadow of growth across his jawline, and a devious look in his eyes, and it was no wonder my knees weakened. I somehow doubted that was the reaction I should have had to a man who was capable of tearing my throat out with ease by the sheer mass of him. He stood just shy of reaching Hendrix's height, he was muscular, and he had a wild streak behind his gaze.

My attention swept from one brother to the next. Caspian was the largest, a bear in size that towered over me. Hendrix was only slightly smaller, but he radiated so much dominance and power, it was almost suffocating. River, though, well, he slightly terrified me more than the other two somehow. There was something in his gaze, something that told me he was the kind to fly off the handle and think about his actions after the fact. But of course, I could be completely wrong. I should be scared of each of them equally.

"H-hi, I'm Syn," I managed to say, holding myself tall... which was still small considering all three of these men stood over six-foot.

"That doesn't answer my question," River said, folding his hands over his chest, though the playfulness of his words sounded more sarcastic than a kind reminder.

"You're a dick," Caspian responded, standing by the fridge, watching everything unfold. "There's your answer."

"She arrived today," Hendrix interrupted, leaning a hand on the kitchen island, seeming to make himself comfortable, while I was sweating up a storm. "I brought her from the Madfur pack to live with us."

River ran a hand through his hair, looking me up and down with a smirk. "Why? Is she our new cock-sucking whore? Has Caspian grown tired of his?" He turned towards Caspian. "What's that girl's name you like, Katie?"

I bristled at his comment, insulted that he'd say such a thing in front of me. *Jerk*. I cleared my throat. "Like I told Caspian, I will not be sucking any of your cocks...ever."

"Oh, she's feisty." River smirked, offering me a grin that should turn me off... when in reality, it did the opposite. "That warms my insides."

"Don't worry, I'm charming at first, but that will pass very quickly," I snapped back, having had my share of comments from difficult customers at the bar, even if it sometimes resulted in me getting yelled at.

"I like her." River smiled wider.

Hendrix never took his gaze off me. "It didn't take you long to win over Caspian, judging by the fact that you're standing in front of me. Maybe I underestimated you."

I tensed, my gut churning as I felt as though he was setting me up and wouldn't believe anything I said.

Caspian approached me, unscrewed the lid from the water bottle, and handed it to me. "It was my decision," he responded to Hendrix. "If she was truly a prisoner, brother, then she'd be in the dungeon in the basement, not in the room with the best view of the ocean."

With all three men watching me, I felt like I'd stepped into the lion's den and I was the sacrificial lamb. I feverishly gulped down half the cold water, cooling the heat that burned through me from feeling cornered. It also gave me a chance to work out my next move while Hendrix looked ready to haul me back upstairs.

I couldn't help but admire them, though. These brothers were easily the most beautiful men I'd ever seen in my life. Their presence alone already had me instinctively sticking my chest out, making me worried that I might have lost my mind.

Hendrix swung toward Caspian. "We have staff to deliver her anything she wants in her room."

Caspian rolled his eyes. "Chill the fuck out. I was giving her a tour of our mansion."

River shook his head. "I'm still not sure what's going on here. Why is she now living with us again?"

"Because Hendrix took her as payment for the late dues from the Madfur pack." Caspian's jaw set rock hard.

River nodded his head, the corner of his mouth twitching into a tight curl, like the idea of me being here conjured all kinds of ideas I didn't want to know about. "Okay, so she's ours to do as we please?" He sauntered closer to me, studying me, so close I breathed in his masculine cologne.

I squared my shoulders, my breaths rushing at his words. I hated when people spoke for me like I wasn't even standing in the room. Asshole.

River stuffed his hands into the pockets of his jeans. "I can work with this."

What the hell was that supposed to mean? I learned long ago to bite my tongue, but with these three, it was becoming harder to do, even with them being way more dangerous than anything I'd come across in my pack.

River's gaze invaded every inch of me, and the temptation to fold my arms over myself would only mean he won. Under his scrutiny though, my cheeks heated up, burning with embarrassment.

"Oh, she's blushing. She is just too adorable. Who gets to break her first?" River asked with a bit too much glee in his voice. "Please, let it be me." River moved to the fridge to collect a bottle of water for himself.

Hendrix cleared his throat. "Stand down, River." He closed the distance between us and collected me by the elbow. "Let's go."

I resisted him, digging my heels into the tiled floor and

wrenching myself away from him. "I want to see the house, please. If I am going to be living here, shouldn't I be privy to where everything is?"

A strangled snort came from Caspian. "She has a point."

I could kiss him right now for standing up for me. And I might be pressing my luck, but I wouldn't give up. The idea of living with them worried me a lot, so the thought of fleeing at the first chance I got played on my mind.

"If you want me to live in this mansion, then you should give me some liberty. Weren't you the one who said you wanted me to be happy? Well, being locked in a room doesn't bring me any happiness."

I didn't belong here... in truth, I had no idea where I belonged, but it wasn't with deadly Alphas either.

"Liberty?" he snarled. "You seem to be under the illusion that you have free reign. I own you, and I'll decide what you can do."

"I bet you're a pretty wolf, aren't you," River interrupted. "Let's take her out hunting. I want to play."

"No!" Hendrix boomed.

I gasped at his sudden voice, a chill zipping down my spine. When Hendrix met my gaze again, I found his eyes had changed. The deep blues were sharper, almost darkening, and red sparks were visible, as though his monster wolf was trying to come through. I wanted to scream at him, especially after he spent so much time showing me around town, spoiling me only to keep me closed up so I couldn't go out.

"Do what you want with her, then," River muttered and strolled out of the kitchen, throwing over his shoulder, "Just let me know when it's my turn to play."

Over my dead body. I gritted my teeth at his flippant remark.

Caspian, on the other hand, had a shoulder against the refrigerator, arms folded across his wide chest, watching everything. Part of me wondered if he stayed just in case his brother went off the rails with me.

"I want you protected," Hendrix told me, his voice tamed down.

I gave him a sickly-sweet smile, not sure what to believe now.

"Then maybe I don't need to keep being locked up in my room? Please, Hendrix. I can stick to the house only, and one of you will always be watching anyway."

His brow furrowed, and he huffed. Darkness swept over his face so fast, I regretted asking him.

He grabbed my elbow once more, a lot more roughly this time, and hauled me out of the kitchen. I almost tripped over my feet, staring back at Caspian, pleading for his intervention, but he just stood in the kitchen, watching. His mouth tightened, but he never said a word.

I immediately began to kick myself for believing he'd go against his brother for me. He'd just met me. It didn't matter that I'd thought I'd felt a spark...or whatever that was. I was a toy to them... just as River had said. Sure, he had me living in a spectacular home that came right out of movies where cartel drug lords lived, but a prisoner was still a prisoner.

I stumbled into my room, Hendrix charging in right after me. I recoiled until my back struck the wall, my heart trying to break out of my chest with how furiously it thumped. He shoved a hand to the wall over my shoulder, caging me in.

"I'm not a man to defy," he growled. "I'm really trying here."

He towered over me, and he was so close I noticed the red flecks even more in his deep, blue eyes. His lips were full, and it was ridiculous that my thoughts played with the fantasy of what they tasted like rather than escaping this mad man.

"I-I did nothing wrong."

His upper lip curled. "Turn around," he ordered, to which I gaped at him, not moving.

"What are you going to do to me?" I asked softly, and then glanced quickly to the open door behind him, wondering how far I'd get before he caught me.

"Turn," he told me once more with an authoritative tone that said he wasn't going to ask again.

I had no idea how this was going to end, but my body hardened as if expecting his blows. Yet at the same time, a burning heat erupted in the pit of my stomach, excitedly anticipating that he might do something else to me. I'd never reacted this way to anyone else before.

So, I did as he asked, showing him I could follow orders, even if every inch of my body screamed to defy him. A burning heat erupted in the pit of my stomach at how close he stood over me, how his addictive musky and earthy scent flooded me.

His chest pressed against my back, pinning me to the wall. His hot breath danced across my ear, and my breath hitched.

"Good girl."

The feathery touch of his fingers stroking down the side of my body and over my hips had me gasping for air. When his large palm grabbed my ass, a small moan slipped past my lips. He squeezed tight, his fingers pressing between my cheeks.

He gave a small noise of approval. "You're ours, Syn. Remember that."

"No," I murmured a response I never should have voiced. Maybe the fog of how turned on I was made me foolish. "I'm nobody's."

He hastily spun me around to face him, and there was something terrifying and captivating about his deepening frown. "That's where you're wrong." The harshness of his tone reminded me of how he spoke to the flight attendant on the plane.

Hendrix wasn't a man who took being challenged lightly... he was the wolf who'd tear your throat out for even a small mistake.

I tensed, yet for a ridiculous moment, I let my gaze roam over his handsome face, taking in how truly small I was next to him. And I imagined what it might be like to have a man like Hendrix fuck me. Brayden had been my first and only, and at the time, I looked to him like he was my world, like I was the luckiest person in the world. Well, that fairy tale proved to be a complete disaster.

But with Hendrix, I felt different. From the first time, my attraction was instant, even if he controlled me...along with everything else around him.

"You tempt me," he growled, his voice drawing me out of my thoughts and making me focus on only him. "And you push me. But I'll only remind you once. What I say goes under my roof. No disobedience, no anything unless I asked for it."

His words roared in my face, but I found my attention split between his threat and the desire he enticed with the gentle stroke of his fingers across my neck as he seized my nape.

"Next time you go against my orders, I won't let you off with a warning. There'll be consequences."

Fire soared through me from the anger he stirred within me, from the arousal curling between my thighs. I hated myself for feeling anything other than pure fury at his dominance.

But when that moment of silence stretched between us, and his eyes fell to my lips, everything froze in time.

He leaned in, and his lips pressed against mine.

That was the exact moment I lost myself to him. When a fire rushed up my back, when I felt so safe against him, that I softened against him.

He held me by the back of the neck, and our lips crushed.

He kissed me hungrily like he'd been building up to this moment, like the world revolved around us. Stars danced in my vision, and I couldn't breathe, couldn't think.

Hendrix was everything at that moment. My oxygen, my deepest desires.

His body pushed flush to mine. The thick erection in his pants nestled against my stomach, his body on fire. I fisted his shirt and kissed him back just as savagely, knowing my lips would bruise, but I didn't care.

Pushing his tongue past my lips, he invaded my mouth, tasting all of me, coaxing a moan out of me.

Kissing him was almost like flying... I never knew any different with Brayden, but with Hendrix, he had me burning up, and when I clenched my thighs together, the most beautiful tingling sensation moved into my stomach, buzzing through me.

His hand slid under my shirt, tracing a path to my breasts. I grasped him tighter. Soft touches trailed under my bra, so soft I started to tremble. When he cupped my breast and squeezed it tight, I gasped against his mouth.

Excitement shivered all the way down my spine.

His fingers slid down past my stomach and to the apex between my legs. He stroked so lightly, over the fabric of my pants, that I could barely breathe. I gasped against him, small sounds grazing over my throat when I should be shoving him aside. My body betrayed me.

And just as quickly, Hendrix abruptly broke away from me. The wildness in his expression and the bulge in his pants confused me. Why had he stopped?

"That's enough. And that's what you get for disobeying me." He looked at me, his eyes half-lidded.

I reared back. Was he kidding me? I should have known better... After all, I just kissed a warlord who killed people and threatened me. He didn't even ask for my consent, and while heat scorched between my thighs, losing myself to him should have scared me, not made me lose my head.

Raising my gaze, I said, "I-I shouldn't have kissed you, anyway."

He leaned in closer, taking hold of my chin and lifting my head to face him. I trembled while still floating high on the arousal he'd brought out in me just from a kiss. It was a moment etched on my mind because Brayden had never kissed me to the point where my toes curled.

Hendrix sniffed the air, and his wolf eyes glowed with arousal. "You want me."

Great. The big bad warlord smelled my heat. But instead of shying away, I held his stare and brazenly... maybe foolishly, said, "And by the bulge in your pants, you want me too, but that doesn't mean we should act on it."

He chuckled. "You've been hiding that wicked tongue from me. Let's hope it doesn't get you into more trouble." And with that, he released me and marched out of the room. He shut the door behind him, the click of the lock bringing me back to reality with a crash.

I collapsed against the wall, and I could finally breathe deeply.

What the hell was I doing?

I threw myself onto the four-poster bed, the sheets smelling as fresh as a field of roses. That old futon in my apartment never smelled this good even after I scrubbed it thoroughly.

Torn on how I'd ended up on this island and then kissing Hendrix stirred in my thoughts. Staying in the compound terrified me. If the other two Alphas were anything like Hendrix, this island was going to be nothing but aggression and death. Yet my body and wolf reacted to them like I was in heat.

Where could I even go, though, if I did manage to escape?

I remembered Brayden talking about Reject Island, where unmated and unwanted females were sent. The thought of ending up there scared me worse... I curled in on myself and grabbed a pillow, then hugged it to my chest and shut my eyes.

Tension built in my chest, yet I swore I could practically still feel Hendrix's lips against mine. His scent remained with me. My heart squeezed at the wave of yearning he'd awakened in me.

I closed my eyes and let the exhaustion take me.

A knock came at the door, and I flinched, my eyes flipping open. Darkness enveloped my room, a cool breeze streaming in from the open balcony doors.

I must have fallen asleep.

Another knock and my pulse kicked into a frenzy. Had Hendrix returned to teach me another lesson... to kiss me again? Except, with this being their mansion and them being Alphas, they wouldn't knock no matter if it was day or the middle of the night.

"Come in," I croaked and pulled myself off the bed, patting down what I could just imagine was terrible bed hair.

A maid walked into my evidently now unlocked room, pushing a trolley on wheels, plated with food. She flicked on the lights, stealing the night.

"Excuse me, Miss, but Hendrix has ordered I bring you your dinner," she said formally.

"I'm not hungry," I responded in a quiet voice, thankful it wasn't Hendrix. After everything that happened today, I wasn't sure I could take any more surprises.

The girl, who was maybe seventeen or eighteen, shrugged and kept on pushing the trolley across to the table in my room. She had a messy bob the color of wheat, her cheeks covered in freckles, and in her cream dress and white apron, she looked adorable. She was beaming with what appeared to be excitement. There wasn't any sign of her having bruises or being mistreated by the Alphas here. She didn't even lower her eyes but looked directly into mine.

"That is a shame," she said. "My mother makes a killer twice-baked potato. Best I've ever tasted. It's Hendrix's favorite too, did you know?"

I watched her set three filled plates on the table, each full of food, and when the aroma reached me, I couldn't help myself. My stomach growled, and I got up off the bed, then approached the meal.

Baked potato on one plate, and there was enough to feed two people, except by the cheesy, garlic smell, I knew I'd eat it all. Back in the Madfur pack, I'd never been able to eat enough. I'd gone to bed on an empty stomach more times than I could count.

On another plate were slices of steak and vegetables, and on the third plate was a slice of apple pie with a big dollop of cream on top.

"This looks amazing," I practically groaned. "Did you say your mother made all of this?"

The girl beamed at me, smiling with pride. "Wait until you taste it." She set a table setting with cutlery, and then she filled up a glass with what smelled like orange juice. "Don't make me wait," she said. "Sit down and tell me what you think?"

"You don't need to ask me twice," I said, and I pulled the chair out, making myself comfortable. Picking up the fork, I tried the potato first. How could I not?

The moment it touched my tongue, the food melted and flooded my mouth with the most incredible flavors. Creamy and cheesy with a hint of garlic and something else I couldn't work out. But it was so unbelievable, I kept on eating it, unable to stop.

The girl laughed. "Told you."

I glanced up. "I could eat just this for the rest of my life. Sure, I'd end up looking like a potato, but how can this taste like heaven? And there's a flavor in here that is magic, but I can't work it out."

"Nutmeg. Don't tell her I told you, but it makes all the difference."

I kept shoveling into my mouth as she watched me, and guilt rose through me. "Sorry, I must look like I've never eaten in my life. Take a seat, join me."

She glanced at the doorway and back at me. "Are you sure? I would like that."

I smiled and nodded, to which she rushed to the door and pushed it shut. Then she took a seat across the table from me, grinning.

"My name's Eliza," she said. "I work here with my mother. She makes delicious meals and I deliver them."

"I'm Syn," I replied and quickly drew the other plate in front of me to try. I stabbed my fork into the green beans tossed with roasted walnuts. "I arrived here today," I admitted slowly. "And I really don't know yet what's going to happen to me."

Eliza offered me a lopsided grin. "I'm sure everything will be okay. Hendrix is a very generous man who cares for his pack."

I almost choked on my food. "Are we talking about the same person?" I half-joked.

She smiled at me warmly. "I understand. He's a scary man to anyone who crosses him. But he has never been anything but kind to my mother and me. When my father died in a traffic accident, Hendrix gave us a home and job on his island."

"And you are okay with what he does?"

She shrugged. "Aren't we all a little bit broken?"

I laughed as her words fell into place in my mind, the truth a bit too close to home. "I guess. Now, are you going to help me? There is a lot of food here."

"Oh, I don't want to come between you and cheesy potatoes." She giggled but reached back into her trolley and poured herself a glass of juice too.

I laughed. "The food I grew up eating was nothing like this. If it had no taste, that's what I got for my meals. But I'd gotten used to it, and it's kind of blowing my mind tasting real food again."

"If there's one thing I can guarantee you, it's that you will be well fed here at Isla de Sangre."

I found myself relaxing around her. She spoke calmly, was a bit too excited over food, which I loved, and she was friendly.

"How long have you lived here?" I asked as I took a mouthful of the steak. I might have moaned out loud, earning myself another giggle from Eliza. How could this food taste this good?

"Almost five years," she answered. "And there are lots of perks. Like once a week, we get off, and all the staff go to the beach for the day and swim and eat. You'll need to come with me next time. There's coral, and the most colorful fish swim there."

"That sounds heavenly, though I must warn you. I can't swim."

She didn't even bat an eye at me. "That's okay. I'll teach you."

Who was this wonderful girl? She was the kind of friend I'd always dreamed of having.

"I'd like that a lot." I continued eating while a sense of warmth flared over me. Perhaps not everyone on this island was a crazy-ass possessive or dominant.

"Did you know that most people on the island are talking about you? Word spread fast about the new girl permitted to live in the mansion with our Alphas." She hesitated at first, then said, "You know you're the first female Hendrix has allowed to stay in his house."

What the heck?

Throat tight from the news that took me off guard, I dropped my fork a bit too fast. It clattered against the plate and vegetables, making a loud bang.

"Oh, I'm sorry." She hastily got to her feet to collect the beans I'd managed to throw across the table. Rapidly, she picked up every last piece.

"It's okay. It's my fault." I helped clean up the mess, and she wiped down the table with a rag, then tucked the mess onto the lower shelf of the trolley.

"I shouldn't have said anything," she said, already on her feet and collecting her trolley.

"Eliza, it's okay." I got to my feet. "You did nothing wrong. It just surprised me because I don't know exactly why I'm here. Before yesterday, I didn't even know Hendrix existed."

She nodded, her cheeks reddening. "I think I should go back now. Mother will send a search party out for me otherwise. I'll return later to collect the plates." She pushed the trolley to the door and looked back at me over her shoulder. "It was really nice meeting you, Syn. I don't have many friends here."

"Maybe we can be friends," I said.

With a shy smile, she hurriedly left my room, the lock clicking in place, and suddenly I felt confused. What was that all about?

Inhaling sharply, I tried to shake off that paranoid feeling running up my spine. Coming into the compound, I'd seen lots of women... mostly naked, but they looked like they lived in the mansion. Except they didn't. So, why did Hendrix insist on putting me in this room then?

Standing up, I walked outside onto the balcony where a cool breeze blew through my hair. Tiki torches lit up the pool area downstairs where I spotted River diving into the crystal water lit up by underwater lights. There were women down there too, only in bikini bottoms.

I chewed on my lower lip, part of me wishing I was that brave. But with the scars on my back, I wouldn't ever dare go out in public exposed. There was a reason Brayden rejected me...he couldn't stand that I wasn't perfect. He was embarrassed by me.

I tried to shake away the horrible feelings settling in my chest. I'd dealt with them most of my life, but for some reason, seeing the beautiful women surrounding the Alphas made me more aware of my imperfections.

I watched River swimming. He'd done about twenty laps of the long pool when he eventually climbed out. My gaze instantly dipped over his body, the muscles in his back, his strong legs, and how his shorts clung to his ass. The man was built, and from up here I could just make out some of the tattoos across his back.

A blonde rushed over to him. They chatted closely, then he placed his hand on her breast, squeezing it.

My reaction froze me all over, my heart thundering at spying on them in their private moment. All the while, my nipples tightened painfully against the fabric of my bra as I squeezed my thighs together. He whispered something in her ear as he trailed his hand down her stomach and slipped his fingers under the elastic of her bikini bottom.

I found myself leaning forward to hear his words, while every part of me thrummed with my heartbeat.

The woman moaned, and I couldn't help myself. In my mind, I imagined me being the blonde pressed up against his chest. To have his words in my ear, his fingers touching me. I swam in a growing need, in burning jealousy. And River was giving me a reason not to look away, the longer he kissed the woman, fingering her out in public.

I couldn't stop myself from staring.

Without warning, River raised his gaze, and looked straight at me, grinning. Like somehow he'd known I was watching him this whole time. And he never stopped fingering the girl.

I flushed instantly and practically threw myself into the room. Madly, I drew the curtains shut then pressed my back to the wall, admittedly breathless.

Shit. Shit. Shit.

I shouldn't have been spying, especially when I knew how deadly these Alphas were. River had already hinted at me being a plaything. Seeing me practically in heat watching him was only going to give him the wrong idea.

And yet, I was so wet and turned on that I marched right into the shower...hoping for just the right water pressure.

RIVER

A piercing scream wrenched me out of my sleep.

"What the fuck!"

I jolted to my feet, the bedsheet tumbling to the floor while I sucked in sharp breaths. I tried my hardest to keep up with the whiplash of leaping out of bed at lightning speed.

My brain wasn't catching up quick enough. I darted to the balcony in my room, half expecting someone to have been murdered in the courtyard.

The grounds were silent; the only movement was the two guards down by the front gate.

I stood out there in the balmy breeze, waiting for another sound, but nothing came.

Retreating to my room, I glanced down at the clock on the bedside table. Just after midnight... What the hell had I heard?

Or was it all in my head... Another damn dream? I sighed loudly because I thought I'd put those behind me.

I rubbed my eyes, seriously starting to believe I was losing my shit. That wouldn't be the first time I woke startled, sweating, and my heart pounding like a fucking drum was counting down to my sacrifice.

I grabbed my boxers off the floor from where I'd dropped them, pulled them on, and padded out to my hallway, curious if anyone else had gotten up.

Nothing stirred, and darkness consumed the mansion. I frowned, convinced the sound was in my head.

Then again, my brothers were at the far end of the hall and both slept like fucking bears. Nothing woke them up.

And I figured since I was up, I might as well get a drink from the kitchen. Barely a few steps out of my room and the scream came again.

It sounded strangled, like they were gurgling.

That sure as hell wasn't in my head. It came from the other end of the hallway... where Syn slept.

My gut tightened, and I threw myself in that direction. I spent the time picturing someone in her room, attacking her. We had enough men without mates in our pack, each one of them desperate for unmated females. So what if one of them... I'd skin them alive.

At the thought, my wolf stirred just below the surface, ready to pounce out while my mind roared.

I barely knew the girl, but I wasn't blind; I understood why my brothers were tripping over themselves for her attention. She was breathtaking, but I was a realist and knew that anything good didn't last long.

Yet, *look at me*... I ran like a lunatic to her rescue. I shoved at the door handle. Right, locked.

Fuck. I rammed a shoulder hard into the door, and the splinter of wood snapped, the door flinging open from my force. It swung out wide and smacked into the wall as I charged into the darkened room.

I growled, scouring for the intruder.

Syn gasped, and the shuffling sound on her bed had me charging toward her.

But I came up short on finding an intruder. No one had broken into her room.

She was sitting up, clutching the blanket to her chest, a panicked look in those spectacular green eyes.

"River!" her voice quaked. "W-what's going on?"

My head pounded, trying to make sense of what I'd heard since it sure as fuck wasn't marrying up with the image in her room.

"You screamed. Someone was hurting you."

She stared at me perplexed, having no idea what I was talking about. "No one's in the room but you. I...I woke up with a scream in my throat," she finally admitted. "Maybe that's what you heard. I didn't mean to wake you."

My mind blanked as I ran her words through my head. "What were you dreaming about that made you scream down the whole mansion?" I did my rounds through her room, double-checking the bathroom, the wardrobe, and even under her bed. All clean.

"Sometimes I dream of bad things," she murmured. "But it couldn't have been that loud since I don't see anyone else literally tearing the door down to reach me. Oh, right, you've already done that." A teasing tone played on her words. Was she patronizing me?

When I returned to the side of her bed, the moonlight from the window lit that beautiful little face and distracted me from my thoughts. Pursed lips, large eyes, and cheeks so flushed from being surprised by me. It made me wonder if she'd blush that hard when she was being fucked.

Even the darkness in the room couldn't conceal my appreciation for someone as spectacular as her. A sweet, feminine smell filled the space, and I caught sight of her bra hanging off the back of a chair near other clothing. Of course, she wore nothing under her pajamas, and it had my cock stirring.

I ground my jaw, reining in my wolf. He groaned within me, delighting in her scent.

She drew in a steady breath and stared at me sharply.

"Tell me about the bad things?" I asked. "Did someone hurt you?"

She blinked at me. "Why do you care?"

Okay, her standoffish reaction wasn't a surprise. And I did just break down her door, probably scaring her half to death. I sat on the edge of her bed, drawing in a knee, trying to look as unimposing as possible. I probably shouldn't care, but part of me did. I yearned to learn what plagued her dreams.

"I'm not a stranger to nightmares," I told her.

"Doesn't everyone have them?" She tried to act as nonchalant as possible, even if her hair was in disarray and she looked like she'd tossed and turned all night, so she wasn't fooling anyone.

"Gorgeous girl, sorry to say, but the way you practically screamed bloody murder, that wasn't normal. I should know."

Hendrix once made me go see a counselor, saying he was tired of me waking him up in the middle of the night with my shouting. Sometimes he'd find me sleepwalking. The night we moved to the island, he tracked me down in the ocean up to my waist, shouting for everyone to leave me alone apparently. I laughed at the memory years later, though at the time, I had been terrified. If Hendrix hadn't found me, I would have kept on walking into the sea until I drowned.

Grabbing her pillow and hugging it to her chest, Syn shuffled back in bed and crossed her legs in front of her. She licked her lips nervously, and something about how shy and delicate she looked, so breakable, made me want to madly protect her. To take her into my room, watch over her as she slept, wake her when her nightmares started.

Listening to myself, I wanted to kick my ass. Fuck, I had never brought a girl back to my room. That was my sanctuary, and yet for Syn, I already dreamed of keeping her there.

Fuck me. I barely knew her and already found myself behaving like my brothers.

What had she done to us?

"Tell me about your dreams, and I'll tell you mine," she offered in a brazen voice that suited her. Plus, there was something comforting in talking about the broken things that came to us in our dreams while both of us were shrouded in the night.

This was the girl I'd seen down in the kitchen, the one I'd been watching around the compound the last few days when Hendrix had allowed her to walk around... because there was a reason I was the best spymaster anyone's met...but I was digressing. I'd watched Syn from a distance ever since I arrived back home, and at first, I thought her coyness was an act. Except it wasn't, I realized.

She always looked over her shoulder and studied everything. I let myself believe she might be trying to find a way to escape, but that wasn't the case at all. She was scared. Terrified, in fact; she checked every shadow on her back. The only people who did that were either killers who had every reason to be cautious, or victims of abuse.

I doubted this delicate thing was the murdering type.

"Sure, I'll bite," I finally answered her as she waited for a response. When I went to speak though, my words stalled, not wanting to come out so freely. When was the last time I'd spoken to anyone about my nightmares? About my sleep-walking...both of which had become less frequent over the years.

She looked at me curiously, and it was easy to lose myself as I stared at her. It almost bordered on obsession. And how quickly I felt these emotions around her worried me.

"Are you going to say something, or is this a staring competition?" she teased.

Fuck. Clearly, this wasn't a good sign that I found her so intoxicating. Though, her presence was a breath of fresh air in the mansion... maybe that was why all three of us were so enraptured by her.

Clearing my throat, I said, "It's not something I talk about lightly, that's all."

I noticed her small smile falter, and her eyes glittered with interest. "I know what you mean."

"My father was a fucking asshole. Excuse me for swearing. But we grew up in a home where most days you didn't know if he was going to say hello in the morning or shove you against the wall for getting in his way. It all happened after he lost his mate, you see. Love can really screw you up."

I fell silent after that, my thoughts floating into the past.

"Get in there, you little shit," Father growled, his large hand palming me in the back. He hit me with such force that I tripped into the wardrobe. My forehead hit the back wall, and stars danced in my vision. "Next time you think it's okay to speak rudely to me, to demand anything, I'll break your bones."

He kicked my legs, and I drew them inside, my inner wolf whimpering. I wanted to yell back that I only asked for a second slice of toast for breakfast, and that I was sorry.

But the door slammed shut, locking me inside, stealing all the light.

I yelled, terror squeezing my chest, and banged my fists on the door. "Let me out!"

Of course, my shouts fell on deaf ears, like they always did.

I slumped back in the empty cupboard, hugging my knees to my chest, and blinked the tears away. I rocked on the spot, back and forth. The wardrobe smelled of piss from the last time he forgot I was in here for a full day and night.

"Don't cry, don't cry," I whispered to myself, because I knew

if he came back and caught me, he'd bring out the whipping branch. His words already echoed in my ears, "You're weak. Men don't cry." I cringed, feeling the phantom strike of the branch across the back of my legs. Of course, I'd heal... he counted on it so no one saw what he did to us.

I shook and wished with everything that I was stronger, that he didn't hate me.

When the door finally creaked open, I flinched back. I had no idea how much time passed.

"River," Hendrix murmured softly, his face poking through the open door. "Are you okay?" He had huge eyes that were red like he'd been crying.

I nodded, and that time I couldn't hold back the tears.

"Don't cry," he said. "Here, I brought you something. Eat it quickly." He handed me a sandwich, and I grabbed it before he shut the door, the click of the lock set back in place.

Hungrily, I bit into the meal, eating it fast when I heard the loud thump of footsteps hit the floorboards outside. I jammed the rest of it into my mouth and swallowed it quickly, half of the sandwich stuck in my chest. But I wouldn't risk it... not when it would turn Father's wrath against Hendrix.

Syn cleared her throat, and it pulled me out of my mind. Right, she was waiting for me to explain about my nightmares. But she beat me to it...

"Hendrix told me what your father did to you and your brothers at the lake," she continued. "I'm so sorry that happened to you all. That's never right." She had her hand on mine, her fingers so tender, so comforting. Of course, Hendrix would have told her... she had an aura about her that made you want to open up your soul and lay it out in front of her.

My wolf groaned inside me; the gesture was one of acceptance of Syn. He liked her a lot... a bit too much, perhaps.

"You know enough about me. It's your turn then," I said,

my throat raw, the past still sticking to my thoughts like cobwebs. Memories that haunted my dreams.

Syn faked a yawn. "There's really not much to tell. Just a stupid dream."

I laughed at her. "Don't lie to me," I said, holding her gaze, rather enjoying how easily she distracted me from my mind.

"You sound just like Hendrix," she answered.

I half-chuckled and gave her a cocky grin. "The difference is that I have an innate ability to sense when you're lying, unlike my brother who bluffs."

She raised a thin brow. "Like a lie detector? I've never heard of anyone having such an ability."

"Remember what Hendrix told you our father did to us? Well, something happened that day. Something we still don't understand, but we all changed. My brothers and I are different from your average wolf Alpha. We each gained different strengths when we almost died."

She studied me and gnawed on her lower lip, leaning forward, most likely ready to pepper me with more questions. "I saw Hendrix's monster," she admitted. "What can you and Caspian do?"

"That's a story for another night. I've said more than I should. Now, keep your word and speak up about your nightmares."

She leaned against the headboard and hugged that damn pillow to her chest. Was there such a thing as pillow envy?

"And if I say I'm too tired and want to sleep now?" she said with a slight smile.

I grinned, and an unexpected image crept into my thoughts, one where I crawled into her bed, where I'd lean in and kiss that delicious mouth. I pictured myself ripping off her pajamas and laying her on her back, her breasts glowing in the moonlight as I pushed my cock inside of her.

"You should kiss me then," I said, because that was the first thing that popped into my head.

She laughed and hurled the pillow at me, which I caught with one hand before it struck me in the face. "Get out of my room. I'm not one of your pool girls who are at your beck and call."

The gorgeous angel was studying me, her eyes gazing up and down my body. Did she just notice I wore only boxers? They strained around me the more I pictured myself fucking her.

"I knew you were watching me. That's why I grabbed her. I wanted to see your reaction."

"That's a jerk move," she said, then blew a loose strand of hair out of her face. "Not that I cared."

"Sure you didn't." I shrugged. "But now, you have a choice. Tell me about your nightmare, or kiss me."

In truth, I really didn't need to be staring at her or letting myself fantasize about things that shouldn't come to pass. I learned the hard way that getting close to anyone only ended one way... it fucked you up.

Yet, I hadn't left her room either.

Despite my better logic, in my head, I'd already convinced myself that I wasn't leaving her room without tasting those lips first.

Her brow lowered, and she leaned closer to me with something flaring over her eyes. Something wicked. Her eyes were on my lips. My chest did that thing where it hurt from how hard my heart beat.

She stretched closer, her face so close to mine that I inhaled that radiant sweet scent. Heat flared from her body, and I didn't need to be a genius to know she was burning up for me.

I smiled at her just as she pushed forward, her lips grazing mine. Her breasts brushed against my arm.

Fuck me, but she was everything I'd ever wanted. My wolf growled with a dominating sound of claiming her, making her ours.

Holding back was never my strength.

And the moment this sweetheart broke away from me, smirking and saying, "Done, now you can leave my room," I lost it.

Hell, there was no way I'd leave now.

I chased after her across the bed as she pulled back, and I cupped her face. I kissed her, needing to show her what a real kiss felt like. How she'd forget how to breathe in my presence, how she'd moan for more, how her heart would thrum, and how wet I'd make her pussy. Those were the measure of a fucking incredible kiss.

My cock stirred at her honeyed taste, at the soft sounds she made despite her hands pushing against me.

I never claimed to be a perfect man. Far from it. I had darkness in me. But I wasn't a brutal bastard either, and Syn was a woman who had so much more to learn in life. Innocence radiated from her in waves. And I wanted to be that man to introduce her to everything... to show her the pleasure in life, to make her scream from repeated orgasms.

She might be pushing me away, but her mouth and body melted against me. Either she was confused about what she wanted, or she was too shy to admit that she longed for me to fuck her. My hands combed through her hair, and I held her closer, my tongue piercing past the seam of her mouth. She let me in, sucking on my tongue, and I was going to fucking burst if I didn't strip her soon.

My hands slid to the curve of her waist, and I yanked on the top of her shirt. Our mouths broke away as I wrenched the fabric up and over her head.

Her whimpering sounds drove me insane. She lifted her

head, our gazes clashing as she wrapped her arms around her chest. "This wasn't part of your deal."

"Would you like me to stop, sweetheart?" Bringing her body close to mine, lowering her hands, I relished the fire that leaped from her skin. "And don't ever hide from me. Do you understand how beautiful you are? How when I look at you, I can't think straight. I've tried to imagine what you would taste like hundreds of times already. That's how crazy I am for you."

Her breaths picked up, but she wasn't rushing to get out of the room or put her top on either. I let my fingers trail a line over her collarbone, and to the softness of her breasts.

Silence fell over us, and she just watched me with her huge eyes, but her scent and hard nipples told me exactly what she needed. And it turned me on insanely.

Her breasts were round, a perfect fit into each hand, perky and topped with a pebbled nipple, a dark pink color. I stroked my fingers across them before whispering, "Stunning."

Part of me toyed with the idea of taking her right now, to drown in the heat of her body. But I had no intention of rushing with her. I needed to savor a beauty like her.

She drew her lower lip into her mouth as a wave of arousal slammed into me.

"I promise to be gentle," I said as I leaned in, taking the lead that time. "You'll see."

"Okay," she whispered in a trembling voice, then we kissed, hungrily this time like she'd been holding out on me. I lay her on her back, my hand at the back of her head, while she gripped my arms, savagely pushing her tongue into my mouth. She craved me. And I'd do anything she asked of me at that moment.

Her body shuddered beneath me, and I gave her what she desired. Kissing her firmly, I seized her breast, rolling and pulling at her tender nipple. She responded to every touch, her sensitivity incredible.

I dragged my lips to her neck, where I licked her, and made my way to her ear. "I'm going to eat your pussy now."

A whimper escaped her throat, and every sound she made, every response captivated me. I grunted my approval and made my way down to those perfect tits, taking one into my mouth. They were soft and all mine.

She writhed each time I flicked a nipple with my tongue, and I shifted to gift the other with just as much attention. But I needed something else... and my cock strained, so I slid my mouth down her stomach.

I lifted myself up from the bed, my hands on the elastic of her pants, then I ripped them down her legs, my patience thinning.

She gasped, her breasts bouncing in that delightful way that hypnotized me.

I kept telling myself to be delicate with her, but that was getting harder by the second.

She lay completely naked... all for me. A tiny waist, silky firm legs, and a flat stomach that led a path down to a small patch of dark hair.

I bent forward and scooped my hands under her ass, then I hauled her across the bed until her legs were dangling off the edge. Every inch of her was delectable, and when I spread her legs, she whimpered. I couldn't look away from her plump lips that glistened with her arousal.

Dropping to my knees, I parted her thighs wider, but she quickly covered herself with her hand, making a whining sound.

I kissed the inside of her leg, taking small mock bites, her sexy scent intoxicating and delicious. My thoughts darkened with how wild I felt, how I struggled to hold back from just fucking her that very moment.

When I looked up, I saw her worried gaze. I understood instantly without her having to say a word.

I pressed my lips to the back of her hand. "Is this your first time, gorgeous?"

"Not for sex," she answered shyly. "But it is for a man going down on me."

"That's good, then. I'll be your first, and nothing else will compare."

Her delicate features tensed, and at that moment, a storm of possessiveness swallowed me. She had no idea what she'd been missing out on, but I intended to make it up to her.

I lowered my mouth to her hand and licked it, flicking my tongue between her fingers. She squirmed and broke out laughing just as her hand flinched away.

And I moved in fast, wrapping my mouth around her pussy. I sucked and tasted her, taking everything I'd been craving from the moment I crossed paths with her.

She was divine and didn't come close to what I'd imagined. Just like her mouth, she tasted like honey, but a lot more intense, and a hell of a lot sexier.

A rumble broke over my throat from my wolf as he shoved forward, and I tensed in an attempt to restrain him from taking form. I didn't need to scare Syn... just yet. Next time, if she was a good girl.

I drew in her scent sharply, loving how it fogged my head.

The thrill of being buried deep against her pussy had my balls tightening. I licked and kissed her, then I sucked down hard on her clit.

Her cry grew, that pretty little body thrashing on the bed.

Syn's moans were contagious. I took long strokes of her pussy, then pushed my tongue into her.

Her cries of pleasure were music to my ears. Her hips rocked back and forth, rubbing her pussy in my face. It was a dream come true and one where I could spend hours. That right there was heaven.

When she started to spasm, and her moans escalated, I

grinned and devoured her savagely, needing her to come all over my mouth so I could lap her up like dessert.

When the sweet scream of her explosion filled my ears, she quickly hid them by covering her mouth with a pillow.

She writhed beneath me, and I never let her go. I licked everything she gave me. With her legs shaking uncontrollably, I flicked her wet heat and savored every moment.

I'd never been more attracted to a person before.

When she finally settled down, I climbed to my feet and snatched the pillow from her face, licking her cum from my lips.

She wore an expression of utter passion, her green eyes bright, her curvy mouth curled into a smile. I intended to make her look like this more often.

"That was crazy," she murmured, her voice slightly husky. "I've never..." She gasped. "I've never felt anything like that before." Despite her words, she challenged me with her lifted brow. "But I want more."

I noticed her hands were clenching at the sheets beneath her nervously; this was clearly outside of her usual behavior.

I laughed and tentatively stroked the inside of her thighs. "I know what you need."

Wide-eyed, she watched me as I dropped my boxers, my cock bouncing to attention. I palmed him a few times, and I groaned from the ache I'd been holding onto.

She sat up and reached a hand out towards me, her small fingers curling around my shaft, not quite closing around it completely. "Are you sure it will fit?"

I hissed as she stroked me several times. "I guarantee it," I moaned, then brushed her hand away. I wouldn't last much longer if she kept that up.

Leaning down, I grabbed her hips and lifted them, then tucked her pillow under them. She weighed almost nothing. "I need your gorgeous ass higher," I said.

"Aha," she said, lying before me, spread. It was an image forever engraved on my mind.

I pushed a finger into her, then two, and she arched immediately. The little thing was so tight, strangling my fingers.

"I'll take care of you."

A beautiful smile spread on her mouth. "Yes please," she breathed, and her request undid me.

Her hips tilted up as I fingered her quicker, wanting her relaxed, so my thumb circled over her clit.

"Please, River," she whispered, her voice lingering with pleasure.

I grinned as her body jostled and breasts jiggled the more I fingered her. She gasped, her pussy so swollen and eager for my cock. She was drenched, and the more I rubbed her clit, the harder her pussy sucked down on my fingers

"River..."

I was about to fuck her brains out.

How could anyone ever walk away from her... how could they resist her? Hendrix had told me something about her and Brayden being fated mates, but he had treated her like a slave at his father's bar. For a fuckwit like that to have an angel like Syn bound to him only to reject her, well, he deserved the death Hendrix never delivered.

It almost hurt me to see someone as spectacular as her neglected by her fated mate. But I shook those thoughts away when my focus was bringing her the happiness she deserved.

And I couldn't wait another second. I slipped my fingers out and gripped her hips, aligning that sweet hole with my cock. Then I pushed into her, slowly at first to get her accustomed.

"Oh, Goddess," she cried out.

"You're remarkable." I inched into her some more, and she was so tight, I groaned with the urgency to slam into her tight core. "Relax for me, angel."

She exhaled and flopped her head back onto the bed. Then I plunged into her, filling her completely. Her breathing sped up, her hands fisting the bedsheet. I rocked into her, stretching her, filling her up.

Arousal dripped from every fiber of my body, my cock thick and hard, my balls tight.

She threw her head back, her body arched, and those ruby nipples tightened. They danced over her bouncing breasts each time I thrust into her. The momentum quickened. I grunted and thrust into her, over and over, my eyes seeing only stars from how tight she squeezed my dick.

"Fuck!" I growled, both of us falling into a rhythm. I bent forward and covered her body with mine, my mouth on her neck and shoulder, taking her into my mouth and biting her. I had every intention of leaving my mark on her, so she thought of us fucking each time she saw the bruises.

She cried with pleasure in my ears, then her body shuddered with a delicious orgasm that engulfed her.

Arousal rushed over me from her beautiful moans. I roared, slamming into her one last time before I flooded her with my seed. I growled, my body tense, and I gritted my teeth as I pulsed into her, flooding her.

We were one, tangled together, bursting at the seams.

"I like you inside me," she said with a husky, breathy voice, drawing my attention.

"I'm going to keep you," I whispered back.

Lifting my head, I met her gaze, and that smile was magical. The kind where she forgot about the real world... where she floated. It warmed my heart.

I pulled out of her while she collapsed back on the bed, breathing heavily. She was a beautiful hot mess. Her hair was wild, eyes glazed over, pussy leaking with my cum.

This sweetheart would become mine. She brought things out in me... possessiveness and the need to keep her close.

"Stay there. And don't you dare close your legs," I told her and made my way into the bathroom where I grabbed a towel and lightly dampened one end.

Strolling back into the room, my angel remained on her back, those sexy legs spread, and her pussy glistening, open for me to see it all. I gazed at her curves in the dark, and if she stayed that way for much longer, I'd be fucking her again.

I leaned over and wiped my cum from her, then cleaned down the inside of her thighs too. Like I said, I wasn't a complete bastard.

Tossing the towel to the floor, I collapsed onto the bed alongside her and dragged her into my arms. "That was incredible," I whispered as she curled against me. Her head leaned on my outstretched arm, and she looked up at me.

"I don't remember the last time I felt this content," she murmured, her glazed eyes already starting to close. "Thank you. I will never forget tonight."

I grinned to myself, and in moments, her breathing deepened.

My angel had fallen asleep. Maybe she hadn't been lying about being tired earlier.

I drew the blanket over us and held her, enclosing her in my arms.

I rubbed her back gently, but there was something wrong with the skin there. I tensed and let my fingers graze over the lines and bumps that felt like healed burn marks. She wasn't in pain, or she would have howled at my touch.

I frowned at the thought of anyone causing her such damage. I wouldn't wake her to take a better look, but I was certain I knew what her nightmares were filled with.

Holding her tighter in my arms, I made a silent promise to myself that I'd keep her safe and protected from everyone.

I rolled over, a smile playing on my lips as the taste of my angel still lingered on the back of my throat. Stretching an arm across the mattress, ready for another round, I patted an empty bed and opened my eyes.

Morning light stung my eyes, but I was more concerned about where my kitten had gotten to.

Dragging my naked ass out of bed, I ran a hand through my messy hair and lifted my gaze to the bathroom. The door sat open, and there was no sound of the shower. Up on my feet, I checked to find it empty, so while I was there, I made use of the toilet.

On the way out, I snatched my boxers off the floor, slipped them on, and headed out into the hallway. The door of her room hung off one hinge. That'd need fixing.

She couldn't have gone far.

I had zero clue how I managed to fall so deep under her spell. But waking up with her on my mind, her scent in my nostrils, the taste of her pussy in my mouth, I was kidding myself if I pretended she hadn't affected me. My thoughts revolved around her and what I had planned for us today. I'd been surprised that I found myself so enamored with this woman.

With the waft of bacon in the air, I headed toward the staircase, because if she was anything like me, the calling of food would mean I'd find her in the dining room.

When Syn's soft laughter floated in the air, I grinned and lifted my gaze to the end of the hallway. Changing gears, I made my way in that direction, curving toward the wing of my brother's room.

I passed my room and turned the corner to find Syn and Caspian standing in front of a painting on the wall, laughing. She had her hand on his bicep and wore her pajama pants and tee. The ones where she had nothing underneath.

A white-hot burning sensation ran over me when I saw them together after what we had last night. She was mine!

My brother stared at her like she was everything to him.

Are you fucking kidding me?

Caspian raised his head, glancing at me, grinning. "You're looking at me oddly. What's up your ass?"

I couldn't help it; I strode toward them, my steps striking the floorboards harshly.

My chest clenched, and something about what I'd shared with her made it impossible for me to see her laughing with my brother. She was mine, and I'd make it so.

Caspian glared at me as Syn met my gaze, her eyelids batting, and her gorgeous smile greeted me.

"Morning," she said.

Part of me wanted to return the grin, to take her into my arms, to forget my brother was there.

All was fine and well if it wasn't for the explosion of lava scorching my insides. The fire to possess her all for myself ignited within me. My eyes funneled on Caspian.

"You okay?" he asked again, one of his eyebrows arching.

"I'll be okay in a moment," I growled. I might as well be flying high on adrenaline, feeling like I'd somehow stepped out of my body, and my wolf took me over.

A wild expression flared over Caspian's face at my approach.

"I have something to talk to Syn about," I said, passing him, my shoulder knocking into his. With my attention on my angel, I took her hand and drew her away from Caspian. "Let's go."

"What's wrong with you?" Caspian asked behind me, but I moved quicker.

"Slow down," Syn said, tugging against my hold, but my grasp tightened.

I couldn't explain the jealousy flashing in my mind, and I couldn't stop it either.

Caspian cursed something behind me, but my head was pulsing too loudly with the pounding of my heart. All I had time for was Syn. Only Syn.

"River, please let me go," she pleaded. I saw confusion and frustration in her eyes, saw anger in the way her nostrils flared.

"I won't hurt you. I told you that last night." I wanted to claim her, to keep her safe. There were too many things in this world, even on this island, that could harm her. She was better off somewhere protected.

Caspian marched up behind us, and I tensed.

I paused in front of my room, shoved it open, and nudged Syn inside. "Angel, I need you to stay here, okay."

She stumbled inside, then whipped around to face me, her eyes wide. "River, what's wrong with you?"

But I shut the door rapidly, locked it, then fisted the key.

"What the fuck, man?" Caspian bellowed and drove his hands into my chest. He was a large motherfucker, so I recoiled a few steps. "What do you think you're doing?"

"She's mine," I snarled back, sucking in air. "So fuck off."

"What the hell's gotten into you?" he barked. "Have you lost your mind?"

Syn was screaming from inside my room to be let out, banging on the door.

I groaned, my upper lip peeling back, my mind trying to process his words. My head was foggy, the jealousy stinging. I just wanted to protect Syn. To share those special moments with her where nothing existed but us two. To have someone who understood what it felt like to live with Hell in your head.

"Give me the key," Caspian demanded, a sneer on his lips. "You're losing control."

"Fuck off," I growled instantaneously. Sometimes it was

difficult to tell which part took over... whether it was me or my wolf.

"Move away from the door, Syn," Caspian called out. I barely had time to move before he threw his heel into the lock. Wood splintered, the crack of the lock telling me he'd broken it. He shoved the door open with a hand.

I roared. "Asshole." Wrong move. I shuddered, my wolf rumbling in my chest, and fury burst through me.

I hurled myself at Caspian, leading with punches.

CHAPTER 21

SYN

I screamed.

After struggling in the doorway, the two brothers crashed to the floor, feet from me, bursting into a brawl. Their vicious growls and punches had me recoiling. They rolled across the room, and it was impossible to work out who struck who with how fast they reacted and attacked. Mind you, they were still in human form, and I could just imagine how terrifying they'd be in their wolf form... bringing back flashes of Hendrix in his.

But what the hell had come over River? Even though I had no clue how I'd let it happen, last night had ended up magical, a night I would never, ever forget. Brayden had never come close to making me feel the things River did. But today, he behaved like a jealous stalker. Like a possessive beast gone mad.

The growls coming from their fight had me tensing and backing away. My body trembled, and my knees softened. I still felt River's kisses on my body, my lips bruised, and the ache between my thighs leaving a delicious reminder of what we'd done.

But this, I didn't understand. And I wanted nothing to do with what was going on.

Caspian tossed River halfway across the room where he smashed into a table, which broke under his fall. Then Caspian darted across the room with lightning speed.

I gripped my middle, needing to get out of here... out of their way.

I glanced at the door and hurried into the hallway, only to slam right into a wall of muscles. Bouncing back from Hendrix, he snatched my shoulders and steadied me.

"I got you," he said, his furrowed brow softening.

A thunderous crash hit the wall from within the room, feeling like the whole house shook.

"The fuck!" Hendrix growled.

He sucked in a deep breath, and I noted the air of danger around him like he could put down both of his brothers if he so chose.

"Syn, stay here."

He guided me to stand aside then stormed into the room. One thing was for sure: these brothers were dangerous; not just to others but to each other.

Stumbling backward, my heels hit the wall, and I flinched at the banging crashes mixed with thunderous growls.

Several guards rushed up the stairs at the chaos. The moment they caught sight of the brothers at each other's throats, their faces blanched and they made a hasty retreat.

Everyone was terrified of them.

It was only when the sounds suddenly died that I got worried. Licking my lips, I approached the doorway cautiously and stepped inside.

Hendrix had River by the neck pinned to the wall, a low growl rolling over his throat, their gazes connected. I'd seen this once before... where Brayden's father, the pack Alpha tried to make a beta male submissive. Anton held the wolf's gaze until he finally submitted.

Caspian stood nearby, watching, wiping the back of his hand across his bloody lip. His hair sat messily around his face, his shirt ripped, but he seemed more concerned than furious.

When a rugged keen whimpered from River, Hendrix released him. He tumbled to his knees and sucked in fresh air to fill his lungs.

"What the fuck is going on?" he barked.

"He pissed me off," River snarled, getting to his feet, shoving the hair out of his face.

"You bastard," Caspian howled. "You attacked me, remember that? Syn is not your toy. You don't get to shove her into *your* bedroom and lock her up."

A guttural growl spilled from Hendrix when he twisted his head to face me. "Are you okay?"

I nodded. "I'm not hurt. Just more shaken."

With his jaw set like concrete, he whipped back to his brothers. "This bullshit ends now. She's not yours to own, River. She's not Caspian's either. Or just mine." He glanced at Caspian, his lip curling up. "She's *ours*. Ours to play with. Do you understand what that means?" he snarled, mostly at River.

My lips pressed tight together, and his words struck hard, leaving me slightly dizzy. How could he say that? Did I mean so little that I was just a plaything?

River's pale, blue eyes flashed in my direction, and for a moment, he looked torn as though he couldn't decide between coming to me or following Hendrix's command.

When his gaze finally swept back to Hendrix, his mouth twisted in a scowl. "This sharing thing would be new for you, brother." Darkness flooded his eyes, matching his heavy voice.

What did that mean?

I blinked at all three of them, the air thick. Then River stormed out of the room. Shadows danced across his face, and he didn't even bother looking my way.

My stomach sank, and I felt like a stranger. Like I didn't know a thing about these men. And yet, I'd let myself kiss Hendrix, had sex with River, and fantasized about Caspian. Maybe something was wrong with me for being attracted to such broken men.

Or perhaps that was all I'd know all my life after losing my parents and brother. After living with my fated mate who rejected me. And part of me couldn't help but sense a strange similarity at that moment.

Was Hendrix pushing me away by being cruel... just as Brayden rejected me?

Immediately I wanted to be sick, and my body was taking over as my heart clenched. I curled my fists by my sides, drowning in so many emotions that I stumbled on my feet from how light-headed I'd become.

Anger. Pity. Devastation. And a hungry desperation to just fit in somewhere and stop being tossed aside.

I swallowed hard, blinking fast to pull back the tears. These men took me, but I didn't owe them anything. Not my loyalty, and definitely not my heart. And if I was just a play-thing, then I knew exactly where I stood. It was better this way... especially after my night with River.

Fewer complications. No commitment.

I barely believed my own lies, but when Caspian and Hendrix turned toward me, I forced a smile... it felt strained on my face and so fake. I retreated from the room, wanting to be alone. To sort out the tangled mess in my chest.

Hendrix was by my side in moments, and I glanced over my shoulder to Caspian heading in the opposite direction to us, back toward his room, I supposed.

"Are you alright? Did River hurt you?" Hedrix asked

again. He was a gorgeous man, one that had drawn me out of my life and into his. Who made me feel things I never expected, but I didn't want to be hurt again.

"No, he didn't," I answered. "It was just a mix-up." In truth, I wasn't sure what it was, or why I was standing up for him, but I hated seeing the brothers fight.

Something on his face changed from a hard expression to one of compassion, which took me off guard. "After this morning, you deserve a bit of fun in your day."

"What do you mean?" My shoulders reared back, and I stared at him stunned. Brayden had often promised me great things, but it always backfired on me and benefited him. So what did Hendrix have in mind?

"Take a shower and meet me down in the kitchen. I'm arranging for Eliza to give you a tour of the house. She spoke excitedly about you the other day."

I straightened, my shoulders pulling back. "Wait, you trust me to leave my room without one of you breathing down my neck?"

"I can't keep you locked up forever." He grinned genuinely, and I looked up at him, wanting to say so many things, but I couldn't find the right words.

I struggled to get his earlier words out of my mind. They shouldn't upset me, especially seeing how I was drawn to all three Alphas. But the way he'd said it sounded like I was nothing. Was I fooling myself that I'd be anything more no matter where I was or who I was with?

"That would be nice." I didn't say anything else, and we separated at the top of the staircase, a tightness forming in my chest.

"This way," Eliza said, waving for me to follow her down a hallway to a part of the mansion I didn't know existed.

After this morning's fight, which still made me feel uncomfortable, I decided to enjoy the tour around the house.

"I'm coming," I replied, rushing to catch up with her. She was just slightly shorter than me but walked fast, her blonde bob bouncing around her jawline. Tucking her hands behind her back, she pulled at the cord of her apron and took it off, then ducked into a side room.

I peered inside the storage room that held hooks on the walls with lots of aprons and coats. The shelves were filled with bath towels, bedsheets, and all manner of upholstery.

"That's better," she noted with a small grin, lightly kicking the door shut behind her. "When you run around all day, the apron just adds to overheating you."

"It *is* freaking hot today. That's why I wore this." I glanced down at a simple, sky blue dress with thin straps and buttons running down the front. The fabric seemed faded now that I looked at it carefully. "It's really comfortable." I patted the crease across my stomach.

"It looks gorgeous on you," she cooed. "You're so pretty, Syn, I hope you don't mind me saying. No wonder the three Alphas drool at you the way they do."

My cheeks flushed, but then I recalled how crazy things got earlier in the morning, and I changed the topic. "Hendrix ordered some things, but everything is too fancy for day to day. I need some other clothes."

"You might get the chance. Once a month, we have a clothes boat come to visit us. Well, that's what I call it, but it's a man who visits a bunch of the islands selling all kinds of clothing. It's fantastic. I bought five dresses from him last time he came."

"That sounds amazing." My mind went for a second to the restaurant where we'd eaten. It had been a crazy experience, but I'd love the chance to actually pick out my own things. I'd never had that chance with Brayden. Although that was in the past, I doubted Hendrix was going to agree to me working to make some money.

"Perfect timing for his next visit. He'll be here next week!" Eliza's smile was contagious, and I thought again how much I liked her. "I can always lend you some of my clothes if you want?"

"Thank you. If I need something new, you're my girl." And we continued our tour.

We reached another staircase at the end of the hall. Not as elaborate as the main one near the front door. This one had black railings and a red carpet running up the middle of the steps that lead to the next two floors.

"The mansion has two wings," Eliza explained. The main one is occupied by the Alphas, and only they are permitted there, unless we are delivering something to them, or we are called. And this wing," she pointed to the one ahead of us, "is for guests." She leaned in towards me, whispering, "But it's never used."

"I thought there were guests all the time for business?"

"Oh, they come for dinners, but they're never allowed to stay over," she explained.

She raced up the steps, and I hurried to keep up. "I come up here sometimes to just get away, and when I need alone time. No one visits these rooms."

On the next floor, a circular corridor surrounded the stairs, and when I glanced down, the hallway came into view. I counted four rooms.

"This is my favorite one." Eliza pushed open the door of the one behind me, and she entered a room drenched in bright sunlight. Through the arched windows, the view overlooked the forest behind the mansion, and the ocean glimmered blues and golds in the distance. Warmth engulfed me the moment I stepped inside. A bed sat against the far wall below a beautiful tapestry of two stags mid-battle, their oversized antlers clashing. A faux white fur blanket lay bundled at the foot of the bed, and I could picture myself falling asleep there with the sun on my face.

"It's so relaxing here." I strolled inside, running my fingers along the mahogany desk, complete with a red, velvet-covered chair. The chandelier dripped in crystals. There was no doubt that Hendrix and his brothers were worth a lot of money.

I joined Eliza, who stared out of the window. "You *really* like this island, don't you?" I asked.

"It keeps me close to my mother, and the world out there scares me a lot more, to be honest. Until I find my fated mate, this is the safest place for me because I don't want to end up on Reject Island. I've heard some dreadful stories from there." She paused for a moment, lost in her own thoughts like she'd experienced a lot more than she let on. "So, what about you? If I can be so bold as to ask, how did you end up here? All the rumors mention Hendrix stole you from your fated mate." Her eyes meet mine, brimming with curiosity behind them. Her smile, though, was authentic like she truly cared.

"My fated mate didn't want me," I said, then chewed on my lower lip. "But he kept me around to do all the chores and work like a horse. Hendrix took me the night he arrived at the bar. It had something to do with an arrangement for my fated mate's father to pay off a debt." I shrugged, and lowered my gaze, not wanting to think about the bar. There was nothing I missed about working there.

The next thing I knew, Eliza was hugging me. She had her arms around my middle and strangled me with how strong she was despite her size. "I'm so sorry that you had such an asshole of a mate. Was he blind?" She broke away from me, eying me head to toe. "I mean, look at you. You are the most beautiful person I've ever seen."

I half-laughed because no one had ever said that to me before. Plus, if Brayden *was* blind, I could've run away sooner.

"It's his loss and our gain. I love that you're here and I've got someone to talk to. Many people are so serious, and any females who aren't mated are sent off by their family to Reject Island or matched with another pack. I'm just lucky my mother begged Hendrix to let me stay. Anyway, enough about that. Come, let me finish showing you around."

The tour went fast, seeing that at least half the rooms in the mansion she didn't have permission to enter, or were locked. And the basement was completely out of bounds, which had me intrigued.

We stepped outdoors through the kitchen rear door, and the sun heated my face. The gardens lay out in front of us, and a tall, lanky man was shoveling dirt near the row of carrots.

"Hi, Joe," Eliza called out.

He paused and glanced our way, lifting his cap out of his eyes. He had short, dark hair, was cleanly shaved, and looked to be in his forties.

"Morning, ladies," Joe said with a perfect row of white teeth.

When his eyes swept to me, something shifted behind them... it went as quickly as it came. I wasn't sure what I'd seen, but I put it down to him not expecting a stranger to be interrupting his work.

"Are you here to collect vegetables?" he asked.

"No, I'm giving Syn a tour. Not sure if you've heard but Syn just recently moved to Isla de Sangre."

Joe wiped the sweat from his brow with his sleeve. "Sorry, I've been too busy." He crossed the rows of garden patches and stuck his hand out my way. "It's a pleasure. And so good to see Eliza with a friend for a change."

I shook his hand, and it was soft, not aggressive at all.

Maybe the problem was me seeing everyone as malicious and out to hurt me when this guy was perfectly nice.

"Thank you. I'm still getting used to the place."

"Well, I'll tell you this. You ever need any fruit or vegetables, I'm the man you come to." His grin spread from ear to ear, and his brown eyes glinted beneath the sunlight. He had an easy expression, the kind of man who looked like he wouldn't hurt an ant if he could help it. Maybe there was hope for the compound after all, especially if Hendrix loosened his control over me a bit more.

"Sounds perfect."

He stared at us, then said, "I've got something for you both." Quickly, he hurried into the garden and vanished into a dense patch of trees. Moments later, he rushed out on fast steps, carrying two large apricots.

"They're ripe and delicious."

I took mine, our fingers grazing, and he paused for a short moment, staring at me strangely again. I lowered my gaze and drew my hand back with the small gift. "Thank you. It looks amazing."

He cleared his throat. "I better return to work. The soil won't work itself." He bowed his head in my direction, tilting his hat. "It was a pleasure meeting you, Syn."

Eliza dragged me by the arm. "Let's go before someone sees us wasting time." She already munched on her piece of fruit, and I did the same. Flavor burst across my tongue. I might have moaned at how good it tasted.

"He seems so nice," I said between bites, then quickly discarded the seed into the yard as we headed around the mansion toward the front.

"Oh, Joe is awesome. Ever since his wife went missing five years ago, he's thrown himself into his work and manages the whole garden, and it stretches acres and acres. So it's a huge job. And he's always so generous and kind. I think he's lonely."

"That's sad." I tried not to think of my parents, of the image of Mom lying on the kitchen floor dead. I didn't want those memories to ruin the moment.

"I sometimes joke with my mom that this compound should be called the broken island because nearly everyone here has come from a damaged background."

Before I could school myself, my thoughts flew to Hendrix and his brothers, and how their father treated them, then I said, "Yeah, Hendrix's upbringing is quite devastating too."

"Not to mention, what happened with his fated mate," she whispered, her eyebrow wriggling.

My legs stopped moving with her words, and I grabbed her hand. "Wait a moment. Hendrix has a fated mate?"

"Had." She grinned just like the other girls at the bar would when they gossiped about the latest drama. I wasn't included in their conversations, but I heard enough whispers to know what they talked about.

"Oh, you don't know?" Eliza's eyes were huge, and she drew me under a tree the size of a two-story house, blossoming with white flowers.

My stomach tensed up, as he'd never mentioned anything about his fated mate. I was deliberately ignoring the flash of jealousy teasing up my spine as I thought about it.

After looking left and right to make sure no one was near, Eliza said, "He rejected his fated mate because she cheated on him. He was furious and kicked her off the island, then disappeared himself for a full month. No one knew where he went."

My heart twisted, and I pressed a hand to my chest to ease the growing tightness.

"Then he came back and pretended like it never happened.

No one dared mention her name, and anything relating to her had to be thrown out."

"Wow." I pinched my lips and an unease creased my brow. He never said he rejected his fated mate, even after knowing what Brayden had done to me. Frowning, I started to burn up with anger that he withheld that from me.

The morning fight between the brothers flashed into my mind. Along with his words about sharing me. My instinct had told me something was wrong.

My gut clenched harder. And I was convinced I'd hurl.

He rejected his mate, and the reason he wanted to share me was because he wasn't that into me. I was someone to have fun with, to pass around.

"It was a big deal, and everyone was talking about it," Eliza continued. "Especially since she cheated on Hendrix with River."

"Fuck," the word slipped from my lips, and a wave of sickness hurled through my stomach. Bile hit the back of my throat as all I could picture was the chaos that went down earlier in the day. River acting all weird and possessive, Caspian standing up for me, but then Hendrix's attack on River.

And his remarks made perfect sense.

Sharing would be new for you, he'd said.

Fury surged through my veins, turning my insides to spitfire. I tensed, wanting to go to Hendrix and ram my fist into his face. He rejected his fated mate and then brought me here, pretending he cared about me.

Fuck him! Though I cringed with the knowledge I had slept with River... Shit, that complicated things.

"Hello, Syn," Eliza said, snapping her fingers in my face. "Are you alright?"

"I-I'm not feeling too well. Do you mind if I go back to my room please?"

Her cheeks flushed, and she nodded. "Of course, right away. Look, I didn't mean to upset you. I shouldn't have told you that about Hendrix."

I took her hand in mine. "You did nothing wrong. I think the apricot is just sitting funny in my stomach. Maybe we can continue the tour on another day?"

"Yes, I would love that." With her smile returning, I did my best to grin when she looked at me until I reached my room Then I shut the door, and a growl vibrated in my throat.

Furious at Hendrix, I paced in the room, tossing the pillows at the wall, ripping the bed sheets off. I knocked the chairs aside. I wanted to hurt him, to hit him.

A headache pulsed at the base of my head the more I went over everything I'd learned.

Hendrix's promises and his insistence that I was special to him made no sense if he happily shared me. Part of me felt like a hypocrite for questioning him, but the fact that he rejected his fated mate, just as Brayden had done to me, hurt. And it made me fucking furious that he never told me.

Unable to tame the fire in my heart and stop my mind from racing, I threw myself onto the messy bed and closed my eyes. Then I counted down to calm myself, to think this through.

I had no clue how long I'd been lying on the bed, but the raucous sound of voices outside had me climbing to my feet and going to the balcony. Night spread over the heavens, and I realized most of the day had passed.

Frowning, I searched the grounds for the commotion. I eyed two guards dragging someone toward the far corner of the yard. The man wrestled against them, and I moved to the railing, watching with curiosity.

The man's cap went flying in the scuffle, and then I saw his face. It was Joe, the gardener.

I shivered, shaking with the feeling that something terrible was about to happen.

I couldn't look away as he thrust against the two men hauling him, but Joe wasn't a big man and stood no chance against them.

Fear crept through me. I could never harm a living creature. Maybe it was something I would work up to if the person deserved it, but these guards were rough with Joe.

They shoved and kicked him, and he dropped to his knees. His hands remained tied behind his back the whole time.

My feet were locked in place, like somehow they were fused into the balcony, because nothing would get me to move while I watched Joe.

What was going on? I hugged my middle as a shiver crept down my spine.

The guards stepped away from Joe, leaving him kneeling on the lawn.

I caught sight of River strolling from around the corner of the mansion and moving toward Joe. He was rubbing his chin, and from my spot, I couldn't hear what they said.

Only Joe's howling cries sounded, and I could tell he was pleading.

One moment, River paused several feet in front of Joe, saying something. The next, he raised his other hand in front of him, holding a gun.

Bang!

The sound ricocheted through the air. And there was so much blood. Joe was flung backward and hit the ground. He never moved again.

I flinched, a cry falling from my throat. "No!"

The horror turned my body to ice, and tears pooled in my eyes. What the fuck!

The sharp pain of grief flowed straight into my chest, and my pulse raced through my veins, through my whole body.

Gasping, I floundered into the room and my legs slackened beneath me. I dropped to my knees and cried into my hands from the sheer shock of what I'd witnessed. My wolf whimpered, and she curled up tight inside me.

My throat squeezed, and each breath grew shallower. I drowned in a cold sweat as terror hollowed my chest cavity.

I wanted to scream.

I had to get out of here.

CHAPTER 10

SYN

I had lived in chaos with the Madfur pack, and some nights, I fell asleep to screams outside my room. It was crazy what you became accustomed to when your choices were crippled.

After everything I endured with my family, with my fated mate, I survived and got away from them. But was life in the compound just the proverbial jumping out of the pan and into the fire?

I'd seen too much death, and I didn't want anything to do with it.

And what if I ended up the same way as Joe? I crossed the Alphas, and the next thing I knew, I was facing down the barrel of a gun.

A cry left my throat as I pictured the scenario.

My head hurt, going in a thousand directions.

I wiped the tears that refused to stay at bay, and I knew the answer. Stumbling out onto the balcony, I sucked in a shuddering breath. A terrifying, hazy sense of panic engulfed me. Along with that sensation of being trapped.

That, in turn, had my anxiety tightening around my throat, while I white-knuckled the railing.

I stared out into the night. Lights dotted the guard posts on the wall surrounding the property, and even down below, those tiki torches showed me where the guards stood from my balcony.

My gaze shot to the lawn where Joe had been shot. And suddenly, my skin felt as though it was stretched too tight over me.

I had to get out of here. That was the only solution.

A few dark shapes bopped on the calm sea--boats and yachts along with a boathouse I spotted yesterday. And it would make the perfect getaway.

Feeling completely out of my element, I wouldn't let that stop me.

Wiping more tears from my cheeks, I made the decision that if I wanted to survive, then only I could make that happen.

I shut off the lights in my room and stepped back on the balcony to not draw attention to myself. And I stood there, watching the movements of the guards, along with the entrance into the compound. That was going to be the hard part... getting past the gate.

The longer I watched, the more I was convinced getting out through that entrance would be impossible. Guards never moved from the top of the wall, or down on the grounds. They would spot me in seconds, and then what? And what if I did make it to the gate? How would I open it if I didn't have a key?

I gnawed on my cheek, rubbing the goosebumps out of my arms and wracking my brain. It didn't help that all I could picture was the gardener being shot. All that blood, and the finality in how quickly he went down.

I needed to get out of here...

That was when I recalled that at Howler Bar, the supplies were always brought in from the rear entrance to the building. So, there had to be something similar here. Hendrix had told me they sent and received supplies to and from the island. And it didn't look like the main gates down below were large enough to take in anything bigger than two people walking side by side, so there had to be another entryway.

Determination zapped through me, both terrifying and exciting that I was going to do this.

So, for the next two hours, I waited and watched carefully as fewer guards remained to patrol the wall. When the tiki lights were finally snuffed out, throwing shadows over the compound, I knew that was my opportunity.

I immediately moved to the edge of the balcony where the stone walls were covered in wooden lattices and secured to the mansion. White flowers peppered the vine that snaked through them.

I combed my hair off my face and into a ponytail, tucking it under the collar of my shirt. I didn't need the wind blowing it and drawing attention.

Glancing down over the balcony, there were thick shrubs that I hoped would catch my fall if I slipped. No one was guarding this area, so there was no time like the present to get a move on.

Shadows covered most of the mansion, so if I was quiet, I wouldn't be spotted. I climbed up and over the balcony railing and nervously reached out to the lattice. My fingers gripped the wooden frame, and I perched the tip of my shoe on it until it felt secure. Moving my other hand onto the structure, I then secured a second foot.

I hung there, my heart beating furiously, as I whispered, "Whatever you do, don't look down, don't look down."

I'd become resigned to the obvious reality that if the gardener was so easily disposed of, there wasn't a future for me with these monsters.

I didn't want to die.

Releasing a long exhale, I lowered one foot, finding purchase, then shifted my hands down as well, and then the other foot followed suit. My fingers were white with how hard I gripped. But I kept on going, taking my time and not rushing.

When the sound of voices came from farther up the path, I froze.

Over my shoulder, I spied two guards talking low to each other, marching past the shrubs. Guns hung off their belts, and I knew they'd shoot and ask questions later.

Seconds felt like hours by the time they finally passed. My muscles screamed with pain, and my fingers were hurting terribly.

As soon as I no longer heard their voices, I hurried down... well, as fast as I could.

When a howl rang in the distance, I flinched and missed a step. Before I knew it, I was falling backward, and I yelped.

I hit the brushes a heartbeat later, the branches snapping loud in my ears as I crashed to the ground. I whimpered, lying there for a few seconds as everything ached. To make things worse, these dumb shrubs had spiny branches that poked me everywhere. I struggled to get up to my feet, moaning as my back started to hurt while I ripped off the broken branches from my hair and clothes.

But I'd made it down and survived. Yippee for me.

Quickly glancing around, the scene was clear, so I jolted to my right... in the opposite direction those guards traveled. I remained close to the shadows near the wall.

The minute I turned the corner of the building, I froze and snapped back around. A couple was beneath a lofty palm tree, kissing. He had her pinned, and she curled her leg around his hip. He grabbed her other leg, wrapping it around him completely. Then her moans sounded, and he was thrusting into her. Okay, I doubt they'd be spotting me anytime soon.

Head low, I bent forward and raced ahead. The most gorgeous smells of baking bread wafted out from a door I passed. It had to be the kitchen. As hungry as the aroma made me, I kept on going. The length of the mansion seemed to go on forever when a stream of voices came from up ahead.

Glued to the corner, I peered around to where a bulging man with no hair and wearing a black apron was dumping wooden boxes on a pallet sitting on the front of a forklift machine. Whatever was in them, they must be heavy. I'd never seen anyone groan and curse so much when working. His white tee was stained with sweat, and his bald head glistened with perspiration.

Across the yard, the gate sat open, but there were two men with rifles standing guard.

So much for that. But I kept watching the bald man. Once he'd loaded the pallet, he threw a huge, grey tarp over the boxes, covering them loosely.

And instantly, I had my escape. Considering he'd been loading the boxes, meant they were being taken out of the compound. I was positive about it.

There was no one else around, and I had to make a move. The man began shouting at someone through the open shutter doors I could only assume led into the back of the kitchens or the storage. I couldn't see clearly from my angle.

When the man finally dusted his hands over his apron and made his way to the driver's side of the forklift, he paused.

My heart might have just had a small stroke with how loud it banged, knowing that I should have run and hidden under the tarp earlier. Then he abruptly turned back to the open doors and yelled something. I wasn't paying attention, I was trying to breathe.

Just then, soft voices came from behind me. The guards... it had to be them.

Shit!

My stomach turned. I glanced over my shoulder to see two figures strolling up the path, closing the distance to me.

I had to do this now.

I slipped around the corner and crouched low, then I darted through the shadows. The pallet was directly in my path. I didn't even let myself think about it too much. As the man walked into the open garage where he'd been collecting the boxes, I threw myself forward. And I scrambled right under the tarp, where I huddled in the corner underneath, feeling more like a mouse at that moment.

It reeked in there like old socks and rat droppings. Eek.

Not a sound. I covered my mouth and nose, sitting impossibly still.

The man's voice bellowed, and he sounded angry at whoever he talked to. Suddenly, the engine croaked like it might die... That would just be my luck.

But we were moving soon enough, the pallet jolting beneath me, the boxes swaying. Sweat poured down my back and face. It was crazy hot underneath, but I didn't dare move.

Not yet.

Holding still, I thought of all the times I'd dreamed of running away from Brayden, imagining going anywhere but being with him. Except for the small problem of the bands he'd placed on my wrist, suppressing my wolf, keeping me prisoner. He kept telling me only he could remove it...and I foolishly believed him. Sure, Hendrix said he'd get a witch to help me, but after what I'd witnessed tonight, there was no way I could remain here.

I'd find another way to remove the bands. I had to... but my priority right now was surviving.

We came to a sudden halt, and I lurched sideways into a box. I grabbed hold of it to stop myself from toppling over.

The grunt of the engine faded, and my ears perked for any sounds. He was driving away, and I was no longer jostling about.

My pulse bounced beneath the surface of my skin, and only when the sound silence, did I dare peel back a corner of the tarp. The fresh air that found me was like heaven.

The gate to the compound had been shut, and the two guards were chatting on the inside of the compound with their backs to me.

As silently as possible, I crept out from under the tarp and then sprinted to a cluster of palm trees on the beach. I hid in their shadows while trying to catch my breath. Remembering the house boat I'd spotted on the shoreline, I started making my way in that direction.

Waves crashed to shore, and with the sickle moon hanging low, I might have actually enjoyed the scene. The air smelled of salt, and I never had the chance to visit the ocean, yet here I was trying to escape—that was the story of my life.

I looked up toward the wall, not spotting any of the guards, so I darted quietly from one palm tree to another, using their shadows to conceal myself.

My plan was to get onto that houseboat, then hide and wait until someone took it out. Unless I found the keys onboard... I mean, how hard was it to drive a boat? The main thing was just getting out of the compound and praying Hendrix and his men didn't search for me on the boats.

I had no doubt that for too long I had been naive about the world. I trusted the wrong people. But since arriving on this island, I'd seen things that terrified me. And I was completely committed to not being anyone's puppet any longer.

Up ahead, the small dock stretched out away from the

shore... two wooden docks with yachts, speed boats, and the boathouse. They all rocked on the pitch-black sea.

I glanced up ahead to where the entrance gate stood. No guards... maybe they were midway through a shift change. And that meant I had to move.

Shaking, I wouldn't chicken out. Not when I'd come this far. With one final look over to the gate and walls, I jolted forward. Darkness chased after me with a ravenous terror.

My legs pumped as I crossed the white sand and darted onto the wooden dock. The houseboat was in sight. Night shrouded it, but it looked large enough for me to hide in so no one found me.

Fragments of the gardener's death sat heavy with me, and I couldn't shake them from my mind.

Without pausing, I lunged from the dock and toward the boat.

Instantly, an arm wrapped around my middle as I jumped.

A startled cry flew from my lips, and I swung my head around to come eye to eye with Hendrix. He had me in his arms, wrenching me away from the boat.

A scream scratched the back of my throat, and I writhed against him.

His growl rumbled in his chest. "What's your plan, little wolf? Stowaway with the houseboat? You think I wouldn't find you?" The brutal sound of his words flooded me. The heady whiskey scent on his breath....was he celebrating Joe's death?

Anger flared over.

"Are you going to kill me too?" My heart slammed against my rib cage.

His face suddenly twisted with pain as if I'd insulted him. "What are you talking about?" He set me on my feet, forcing me to face him.

Except, I was crying and inconsolable, throwing my fists at

his chest. Plus, I was still furious at him about his rejected mate.

His hands grasped my arms, staring at me with a blazing glare. "Syn, enough. Why would you say that? Because you tried to run? I'm pissed because I told you already you're mine. But I wouldn't kill you for it."

My mouth fell open right then. "B-but River killed Joe, and h-he...I saw it all happen." I choked on my breath. "The gardener was so nice to me. Why did you have him killed?" A tear threaded down my cheek, and Hendrix caught it as it dripped from my jawline, then tender fingers brushed my cheek.

"Little wolf, you've got yourself all worked up. When you have a problem, even if it's with me, talk to me first."

I swallowed hard, my entire body tense as I pulled myself from his grasp. "That doesn't change what you did," I hissed.

Standing in front of him, his scent overwhelmed me, and I hated that he had me drooling when I wanted to punch him in that perfect face. To make him hurt for hiding the truth from me, for having Joe killed.

His gaze dragged from my face to Mateo, who stood to the side of us. His right-hand man. When he looked back at me, his expression tightened. "Let me show you what kind of man I am, sweetheart." There was a twitch at the corner of Hendrix's eye, and he held onto my arm, harder than normal.

"W-what does that mean?"

"You'll see." He seized me by the arm once more and forced me into a march, not bothering to slow down for me. His lips pressed tight as my thoughts filled with images of what he'd do to me...it all revolved around some kind of torture. I felt it in my bones.

He said nothing but walked us right through the front gates, and I had a terrible sense of déjà vu from when he first brought me to his compound.

Darkness crashed into me that I wasn't going to like what he had in store for me. I just knew it.

"Shut the gates, triple the guards," Hendrix's bark at the stationed men had me flinching. "How did you get out?" He turned his attention to me, his head lowered, gaze fixed on me. A low growl in his chest followed his words.

Floodlights from the house glinted in his furious stare. His face was all sharp edges and disappointment. "The rear exit. I snuck onto a pallet." I had nothing to hide.

A smile tugged at the corner of his mouth before he scowled and said, "You should've stayed in your room."

"Why do I have to always stay in my room? Why can't I wander freely like you and your brothers?"

I knew I'd said the wrong thing the second he paused, turned to face me, then slipped a finger under my chin to the point of pain and tilted my head back. "Because I care for you."

His words threw me off. I expected something dominant from him, not this.

"This compound isn't exactly safe for someone like you. As much as I ensure everyone falls into line, there are always a few who won't abide. And the problem is, I don't always find out who they are until it's too late."

I blinked at him, and an ache curled in my gut. I had no idea who he was referring to, but I suspected I was about to find out and not like it.

Releasing my chin, he squeezed his hold on my wrist and we were off again. Instead of going into the mansion, we skirted around it, past the pool, and down a side of the mansion. There were trees on either side of us, bursting with huge, white flowers, which were pretty. It was strange to be in a place with its foundations in corruption and death, and yet the surroundings were beautiful.

It reminded me of what Eliza had said about everyone

being a bit broken. The Alphas brought such darkness to a paradise, and maybe that was to balance them out. Light and dark meeting on neutral grounds... Did living in such a heavenly location help tame their beasts?

At the rear of the building, we passed by the oversized vegetable garden, along with a greenhouse. Then we followed a cobblestone path into the woods that carved through the forest.

He never slowed his march, and I lurched alongside him, my eyes wide at him dragging me into the woods at night.

Lights blinked amid the trees from the distance, and it wasn't long before we emerged into a large clearing. Cabins were peppered along several dirt roads. It was a complete little village within the woods. With the only light from a handful of buildings, shadows swallowed up everything else and plunged that place into a nightmarish feel.

I rubbed the goosebumps out of my arms.

Mateo stood by a wooden cabin, the front door slightly open, and light peered out from inside. Near the entrance, we paused, and Hendrix glanced over to me. "There's always a reason why I do something. Nothing is ever as it appears. What I'm about to show you is so you learn never to question me again."

"Whose house is this?" I was captured by the sight of a flickering candle inside the room, my stomach tightening at his words, at how dark the woods were.

"The gardener's."

I took a deep breath, then another, and I felt lost and confused about why we were here.

"Let's go inside," Hendrix said, his hand on my back, nudging me forward.

I stepped inside, pushing the door wider. Smells invaded...musty and something foul flooded the room as if the house had never been aired. My wolf whimpered like she knew something I didn't.

I sighed, taking another step forward into a simple room with a round, wooden table and two chairs. There was a clean plate and cup on it. No other furniture, but in one corner sat several open hessian sacks of soil, alongside his rake and gloves.

Dark timber covered the walls and ceiling, lit up by a light bulb overhead. The cabin had a sorrowful feel about it.

Hendrix took the lead, and I followed him down a darkened hallway where he pushed open another door. Its creaking gave me the shivers. I hugged myself and followed him downstairs to the basement.

That sickly sweet stench grew stronger down there, reminding me of rotting fruit and perspiration.

A flick of light switched on from the small lightbulb dangling from a rope in the ceiling. I blinked to take everything in. The creepy, dusty room, corners crowded with cobwebs. A study desk huddled against the wall with a chair, and around it were all kinds of boxes. The walls nearby had hooks holding ropes, axes, and blades. There were even handcuffs, which dried my throat. Why would a gardener need those... If it was for something kinky, fine, but why were they in the basement? In front of the desk was a montage of images, but I didn't want to move from the base of the steps.

Everything in the cabin made me sick to my stomach, and I didn't even know why.

I bit my lip while Hendrix proceeded across the basement, and I let my gaze follow him. That was when I noticed there was a closed door in front of him. He pushed it up and hit the light switch.

"Syn," he called me, and I understood he wanted me to go to him.

I said nothing, but I also didn't want to find out what was in the room. I skimmed my fingers nervously over my pants.

"Syn," he repeated, louder. "Come over here."

I dragged myself forward, and a savage snarl rolled in my gut... My wolf wanted me to leave this cabin.

I reached Hendrix, and he stepped inside, while I remained in the doorway.

I scanned everything quickly, from the worn-out mattress on the floor to the chain secured to the wall. The stink of piss and something worse. And when I noticed the dark patches I assumed were blood in the mattress... the same ones on the cement floor, I gasped.

"What is this place?" I retreated, unable to stand looking at it a second longer.

Hendrix hit the lights as he stepped out and shut the door behind him with a bang like he couldn't wait to be out of there too.

"Joe was not a good person, Syn. He's one of those deranged people I told you about hiding in plain sight. He had a young girl who'd gone missing from our pack a few weeks ago locked up down here. I will spare you the details of how he tortured her." He deserved so much more than a bullet."

"Did she survive?" I gasped.

"Yes. She's with our healers and her family."

I stumbled backward, my stomach churning like I was going to be sick. To think, I'd spoken to him, eaten his apricot, and even thought he was a nice person.

What did that say about me?

"Shit!" I hurried across the basement.

"Syn." His fast footsteps closed in behind me, but I wanted to get out of here. My heart thundered while tears blurred in my vision as I kept imagining being trapped in that room. Tied up. Tortured by that fucking monster.

But just as Hendrix seized my arm, something familiar caught my attention from the images stuck on the wall in front of the desk.

Green eyes, deep red hair... Me. I was staring at myself in one of the photos pinned to his wall.

My throat constricted as my veins turned to ice.

I wrenched myself from Hendrix's grip and marched toward the desk, finding a photo of me being dragged into the compound by Hendrix. That was when I noticed there were others of me pinned to the wall, along with other random shots. Me up on the balcony. Another one of me standing in the hallway with Caspian staring at the painting.

I was going to be sick.

"What the fuck!" I cried, and I shook so hard that I wasn't sure I could even sleep with the lights off again. "Why are there photos of me here?" My voice quivered.

Hendrix stood behind me and turned me to face him, then he seized me into his arms. I craned my neck up. His jaw clenched tight, staring down at me. Those deep blue eyes captured me, held me when I wanted to run.

His brows furrowed before he said, "I think you were going to be his next victim."

I might have cried out loud, though it was hard to tell when my knees gave out and the room blurred.

Hendrix scooped me up into his arms, and he carried me back out of the cabin.

He set me on my feet on the grass, and the cool breeze did wonders to clear my head. He cupped the sides of my face, holding me close to him. "Like I said before. You are safe. He's gone, and I'll always protect you."

"He deserved to die," I whimpered, shaking.

"Yes, Joe did."

Hendrix stunned me. I found myself drawn to him from the beginning, from his angular jaw to his captivating smile. Except, he also scared me, and he still hid the truth from me about his rejected mate. He still told his brothers I was available to be shared.

I cursed under my breath at how I both craved and wanted to run from the same person. Yet, as he stared at me with blue eyes that sparkled beneath the moonlight, I had no doubt the man would always be dangerous.

He eliminated a real monster and saved me from ending up in that depraved man's cabin. For that, I owed him.

"Thank you," I murmured softly.

He offered me a half-grin, and after what we'd seen, I shouldn't have been studying how perfect he was, how the fire I felt inside for him roared behind his gaze as well. I reached up and stroked his rough jaw, suddenly feeling like it was just us two.

A tantalizing feeling zipped down my back all the way to the heat between my thighs. Call me crazy, but the comfort of him eliminating Joe had me wanting to crawl into his arms and stay there.

I stopped breathing for a moment as the magnetic pull between our bodies wrecked me. No matter what I thought, my body betrayed me around him... and his brothers.

I nodded, and his massive hand rubbed my back, soothing me. "Come, I'll get you back to your room safely."

With no idea what was going on with me and my reaction to Hendrix, I put it down to the crazy night and how scared I'd gotten.

We reached my room quickly, and I strode inside. I heard the click of the door closing behind me and turned to find Hendrix in the room with me.

"What are you doing?" I murmured, confused slightly.

"You've had a traumatic night. I'll keep watch over you so you can sleep peacefully." He stood still like a statue, making no show of leaving. "Better get changed quickly."

I was almost lost for words. Something about his behavior left me speechless, and while I wanted to tell him to leave, I also craved the company. I didn't want to be alone.

So, I rushed into the bathroom, washed up, then put on my PJs, then on bare feet, I padded toward the bed and climbed in.

He crossed the room and shut the balcony door I'd left open earlier. After switching off the light, he carved through the dark room like a wolf, coming right for my bed.

He kicked off his shoes and pulled the sheets aside.

My breath caught in my throat, stuck for words at first. Did he really think he was just going to get into bed with me?

I stared at him, quizzically, even if he couldn't see me. But he didn't seem to care and lay down with me, also getting under the covers.

"What do you think you're doing?" I shuffled to the other side of the queen-sized bed, pushing the blanket aside to get out.

Large, strong hands snatched me around the waist and hauled me across the bed until my back hit his chest, and I was being spooned by him.

"I promised you I'd keep you safe all night." His voice came out deep and rough like he was struggling to remain calm. I wasn't sure this was such a good decision.

I blushed crazily with how tightly knit our bodies were pressed together, and that masculine scent of his undid me. He laid one arm under my head, and his other settled over my hip, almost possessively.

Silence spread between us, and I didn't move. I was too hyper-aware of his fingers twitching against my skin, of his warm breath on my cheek.

My mind wandered to how conflicted I felt--thankful for him eliminating the man who was going to hurt me, but still pissed at him. I also had to remind myself that rejected females like me didn't have dreams coming true. And I had to wisely choose my fights. So for that reason, I said nothing about his rejected mate.... Not yet anyway.

"Everything I do is for a reason, Syn. Don't question me again. I need you to trust me." He leaned down and kissed my shoulder, almost like a promise of a warning. "You are mine. I will fight and kill anyone who dares to come between us."

I tensed against him, and his hold tightened.

"Goodnight, Syn," he said, the words final, and he shifted in bed to settle down, his arms claiming me and keeping me locked in place.

I laid in bed, breathing in his masculine, Alpha scent washing over me. Heat pooled between my thighs while my mouth parched. This perfect man who made me furious also made me feel things I shouldn't.

And against the urges he brought out in me, I somehow managed to not give in to my desires. I gritted my teeth and shut my eyes.

Because I wouldn't give in to him. I wouldn't let him win.

I hadn't left my room for days...and it wasn't because they hadn't allowed me out. Something was wrong with me.

As soon as I'd found out why the gardener had been killed, I'd been pretty much fine with River killing him. The next day, I'd even gone and laid out by the pool with Caspian.

But I'd gone to bed that night...and hadn't had any interest in going out.

The sky was its usual perfect blue color, but it might as well have been hurricane conditions. Everything around me felt tinted grey, like I'd put on dark sunglasses or something. The first day I'd been left alone, Caspian had stopped by to see what was wrong, and I'd sent him away, telling him I wasn't feeling good. Eliza had stopped by with food trays and to try and hang out, but I'd just picked at the food and she'd eventually left. Hendrix had tried to stop by yesterday to order me out of my room, but he'd actually failed in forcing me to do something for once.

Since then, I'd been flipping through books listlessly and sleeping. I was so freaking tired.

There was a knock on the door, but I didn't bother

acknowledging it. Even when the door opened, I didn't have the energy to look and see who it was.

What was wrong with me?

"Syn," Caspian's voice called.

It took all of my energy to turn my head away from the wall and look at him.

But when I did, it was like a shock of adrenaline passed through me. His voice was the same, but the person standing in the doorway approaching my bed was a hideous beast with two mouths filled with fangs that dripped green slime and vibrant red fur all over its body.

I scrambled to sit up, and I screamed, backing away against the headboard like somehow I could push myself through the wall and get away.

The creature held up its clawed hands. "Syn, what's wrong? Calm down," cried Caspian.

And just like that, the creature was gone and Caspian was standing there as if nothing had happened.

"You—" A sob wracked through my body as I stayed plastered against the headboard.

He took a step towards me and the creature was back. I screamed hysterically and he stopped moving.

And then Caspian was back.

In the back of my mind, I obviously knew that something was not right. Caspian's wolf was definitely not a red-furred monster, and a shifter didn't flicker in and out of focus like that.

But the rest of me couldn't comprehend that what I was seeing wasn't real.

Caspian slowly backed away and left the room, and I sat there trembling on my bed, a sweaty, disgusting mess.

A few hours later, Eliza came back with another tray. Her mother had made my favorite soup, chicken tortilla.

I took one look at it and threw up all over my comforter.

Something was definitely wrong.

Eliza ran out of the room, and I was faintly aware of her calling for help. I looked blankly at the pool of vomit in front of me and tried to get up to pull the comforter off my bed.

As soon as I stood, the world spun around me. I stumbled my way over to the bathroom and started vomiting again as soon as I got to the toilet. I heaved over it, feeling like I was throwing up vital organs.

Footsteps sounded behind me, and then a familiar pair of hands was grabbing my hair and pulling it back as my body continued to shake as I struggled to throw up. I'd thrown up so much, though, that there wasn't even bile to get rid of, so my whole body just shook violently as I dry heaved.

"Get the healer," Hendrix snapped, his voice sounding terrified.

I finally stopped throwing up and found myself leaning against the toilet bowl even as Hendrix tried to coax me to get up.

"I want a shower," I whimpered, knowing that I smelled like vomit and sweat.

"I'll help you, little wolf," Hendrix said in the softest voice that I'd ever heard.

He scooped me up, and when I looked up at him to thank him for helping me, a hoarse scream burst out of me.

There was a terrifying beast with a scaly lizard head and yellow glowing eyes holding me. A forked tongue flicked out, almost touching the tip of my nose.

I began to hysterically struggle to get out of his arms as he tried to not drop me.

"Get away from me!" I yelled.

The monster set me down, and I scrambled like I was possessed across the cold tile floor to get away from him. The creature strode over to the shower and fiddled with something, and I watched in horror as his tongue flicked in and out. After a minute, he walked over to me.

"Please don't hurt me," I cried as the lizard creature scooped me up and walked me over to the shower. I was clawing at his skin, but it didn't seem to phase him as he pushed me under the lukewarm water.

As soon as the droplets passed over my face, I was staring at Hendrix again, no sign of the snake spawn anywhere.

"It's going to be alright, Syn," Hendrix promised. I whimpered in response, not understanding what was happening. Was I going crazy? Was I hallucinating? I was fully dressed, and the water soaked through my clothes until I was a sodden mess.

Hendrix gently set me down under the spray that finally warmed up to a tolerable temperature, and then I watch in a daze as he pulled off his grey v-neck and slipped off his black joggers until he was standing there in nothing but a pair of black briefs that did nothing to hide the enormous package he was carrying.

If I hadn't been losing my mind, I more than likely would have been turned on by the sight of his perfect body in practically nothing. But I was losing my mind, so I didn't feel even a twinge of lust.

He stepped into the shower and scooped me off the ground before walking over to the shower bench and sitting down with me on his lap. I leaned against his shoulder tiredly, keeping my gaze averted from him just in case the lizard monster made an appearance.

I was so very tired.

"Your clothes are covered in vomit. I'm going to take them off," he crooned softly, and I nodded against his skin, not even caring that he was talking about stripping me naked.

He pulled at the bottom of my sleep tank top, and I wearily held up my arms to help him get it off, leaving me in nothing but a thin silky bra that was soaking wet and left nothing to the imagination as far as my breasts went.

Hendrix pulled on my shorts next, which were also splattered with throw up, pulling me up with one arm as he slid the shorts off with the other so I had to do practically nothing at all to help him.

I could feel him growing hard against me, a natural byproduct of the fact that he had a practically naked woman sitting on top of him, but nothing about his movements was sexual. I kept my eyes closed as I soaked in the heat from his body and the water gently falling on my skin. He moved over, and I heard the snap of the shampoo bottle right before his hands reached my hair, gently massaging my scalp. I breathed in the scent of the mango and coconut shampoo, trying to calm down my still rapidly beating heart.

"When did you start to feel off, little wolf? Was it just three days ago?" Hendrix asked, his voice low and gravelly.

"Yes," I murmured, my voice exhausted sounding.

He finished the shampoo and then shifted as he grabbed the removable nozzle off the wall. Hendrix used it to wash off the shampoo in my hair before hooking it back into his holder.

I sighed as he repeated the same process with the conditioner.

If all the people who were terrified of him could see him now...

I tried to sit up and made the mistake of glancing at his face, nearly falling off his lap. I watched in stunned horror as his face morphed back and forth from his beautiful face to the snake creature that probably would be haunting my dreams for the rest of my life.

Along with all the rest of my nightmares.

Finally, I blinked and it was just Hendrix again, no sign of the snake creature.

"Hendrix," I gasped, gripping onto his skin tightly. "Help me."

His gaze was terrified as he stared back at me. "I will, baby," he murmured as I fell back against him, too tired to hold myself up.

He quickly used a loofah to bathe me, not lingering on any particular place on my body. After a quick rinse, we were out of the shower, and I was wrapped in a heated towel.

Even with the heated towel, I was shivering, and standing there holding myself up felt like one of the hardest things I'd ever done.

What was wrong with me?

I tried to take a step forward out of the bathroom, but then Hendrix was there, scooping me up into his arms and striding out of the bathroom towards my bed where he gently laid me down. I made the mistake of looking up at him again, and just like before, his features shifted back and forth between the lizard monster and himself.

"It's not real, right?" I gasped as I shut my eyes and tried to block it all out.

"What's not real? Why do you keep panicking every time you look at me?" he asked, anger threaded throughout his voice.

But somehow, I knew that he wasn't angry at me. He was angry at his lack of control in the situation. There was one thing that Hendrix prized: it was control.

There was a knock on the door.

"Who is it?" Hendrix barked.

"It's me," came River's annoyed voice through the door, and I cringed, hating that he was gonna see me weak like this.

"I have the healer," he continued when Hendrix was slow to answer.

Before Hendrix had even said anything, River burst

through the door, a wildness in his gaze that I wasn't used to seeing....at least directed at me.

Entering behind him was a woman I hadn't seen before. She looked young, like all shifters did since we stopped aging in our thirties.

But there was something in her eyes, something that spoke to just how ancient she was.

River was fighting with Hendrix about something in muffled whispers, but the woman must have been able to hear because she frowned at them both. River growled under his breath, and my gaze darted towards him, just in time for him to transform into a specter with shark-like teeth and oozing yellow eyes. I began to scream hysterically, and River pounced towards me, only to be held by Hendrix who wrestled him to the ground.

"Get out," the woman ordered sharply, and Hendrix and River both froze.

"Why did she act like that?" River asked, the monster switching back to his surly-looking face.

"It's happened a few times with me," Hendrix admitted reluctantly.

"Please," I sobbed as this time both of their features transformed. "It's not real. It's not real." I tried to reassure myself, but my brain felt like it was on the verge of snapping, sending me down a rabbit hole I'd never be able to return from.

I was faintly aware of the healer muttering something before pushing past the monsters and approaching the bed.

"Make it stop," I begged her as she studied me intently with sympathetic deep blue eyes.

"What are you seeing, sweetheart?" she asked me.

"Monsters," I gasped. "They keep changing into monsters."

The healer looked back behind her with a frown. River and Hendrix had once again returned to normal and had moved back against the wall farthest from me. I was afraid that at any moment they would turn again, but at the same time, I wanted them here.

The healer closed her eyes, held her hands over my body, and began to whisper a litany of words in a musical language that I'd never heard before. I watched in distressed awe as a vibrant purple light streamed down from her hands, moving into my body. The light felt warm, and I could feel it moving underneath my skin, traveling down my body as she slowly moved her hands up and down it.

She went down the center of me before moving down my arms. When her hands moved over to where the bands on my wrist were, I felt a shock reverberate through my body. "Ouch," I hissed, almost at the same time as the healer whose eyes had flashed open with surprise. She yanked her hands away from me, and the shocking sensation immediately stopped.

"Oh my," she murmured before shaking her head.

"What is it? What just happened?" Hendrix barked, that familiar red glow beginning to appear in his gaze as he threatened to lose control.

"We need to get Miranda as soon as possible. There's a curse on those bracelets," she said in a serious, worried voice.

"A curse?" asked River incredulously. "I thought it was just something to suppress her shift. I've heard of that being done often in the East."

"All of the bands have some sort of magical property, but the magic in this one is designed to kill her slowly. He must've had some kind of trigger built into it that was released in the last few days, and that's why she started to get sick."

Hendrix opened his mouth to speak but closed it as River darted from the room, presumably to get this "Miranda" woman.

"Is there anything you can do until he returns?" asked

Hendrix to the healer. But she just shook her head, her features drawn and tight. "There may be an herb that can help with the symptoms, but there's nothing I can do now that the curse has been activated."

"How-how many days?" I croaked, knowing that whatever was happening to my body was going to end me soon.

"Soon," the healer murmured, and my heart dropped, the chill inside of me deepening as she confirmed my fears. She turned towards Hendrix who had paled in the last few moments as he stared at me in horror.

"I'll go see what herbs I can find and if there's anything in my books," the healer said before leaving the room quickly.

Hendrix's chest was rising and falling rapidly. Thick black fur was appearing and then disappearing across his arms, and the red glow in his eyes had overtaken everything else.

"You're mine," he growled, his beast threaded through his voice. The sound was comforting somehow. I could deal with that monster...just not the imaginary lizard one. "Not even death is going to take you from me."

I'd always wanted to be wanted, and now that I'd finally found someone who may have wanted me too much...maybe a few someones, it was all going to end.

How was that for irony?

It had been another day, and River still hadn't returned with the witch. At times, I could hear Hendrix snapping at people and large crashes sounding out from around the mansion as Hendrix destroyed things.

I didn't have the energy to check on him though. All I could manage to do was be curled up in my bed...with Caspian wrapped around me.

When Caspian had been updated with what was going on,

he'd latched onto me like he was never going to see me again, nuzzling against my throat and gripping me tightly to him. Because he spent most of the time with his face buried against me, I didn't have to see him transform into a monster over and over again like I did anytime Hendrix entered the room.

I drifted in and out of sleep, my body too exhausted to be awake for very long. At times, nightmares would slip through, and Caspian would begin purring against me. The sound would rouse me out of my nightmare and relax my body enough to fall back asleep.

I didn't think too hard about what an Alpha's purr meant. Tomorrow wasn't promised, and he was just trying to comfort me...right?

I had given up trying to eat. Anything that went down immediately came back out.

There was no denying it. I was dying.

"Syn," Caspian barked, the sound coming out desperate and scared.

My eyes opened with a snap. "Hmmm?" I mumbled sleepily.

"Your chest had stopped moving," he said, clenching me so tight against him that it hurt.

"You have to stay with me. River will be here soon. Then everything will be fine. I promise. But you have to stay, Syn," begged Caspian like I had a choice in any of this.

My heart fluttered inside of me as if it was answering him. I'd escaped death so many years ago, you would have thought that the idea wouldn't have been as scary to me.

But the thought terrified me. There was so much I'd never been able to do in my life.

I'd never gotten the chance to fall in love.

The thought seemed superfluous. How could I even be thinking about something like that? Maybe it was because I was wrapped against Caspian right now, and somehow parts of me were still aware of how warm he was, how he smelled, how he felt. Caspian had been a sweetheart ever since our rather memorable meeting.

In a different world...in a different life, I could have easily fallen in love with him.

Hendrix strode through the door that instant, not bothering to knock anymore, and Caspian immediately tensed against me. "Any news?" Caspian asked. "I think—she's getting worse," he finished, like I wasn't there and listening.

"I have scouts out a few miles away. They'll radio in as soon as they catch sight of River. We'll hear from them any time now." Hendrix spit out the words confidently, like the whole world had no choice but to follow his orders.

He stared at the bed...and me, a longing look in his eyes like he wished he was in Caspian's place.

I was going to ask if he wanted to join when I was suddenly hit with a wracking cough. A spurt of hot liquid burst out of my mouth, and I thought I had thrown up again...until I saw the crimson liquid splayed out in front of me.

It wasn't vomit, it was blood.

"That's new," Caspian said worriedly, grabbing a wet cloth and starting to dab the blood off my face. It was a futile effort though, because I coughed again and another burst of blood splattered all over the cloth he had been holding.

Hendrix made a noise, a sound that somewhat resembled a groan, except it was laced with pain.

"It's okay, my beauty," Caspian murmured as he brushed my hair out of my face. My insides fluttered, a mixture of pain...and warmth coursing through me. I'd always wanted to feel cherished like this. Wasn't it a shame that it was going to be at the end?

"Has she taken everything from the healer? Has it helped at all?" Hendrix rushed out.

"She hasn't been able to keep anything down," Caspian responded.

Hendrix grabbed his hair, pulling it with crazed eyes. "There has to be something," he roared as he picked up a vase, turned around, and threw it against the wall, shattering it into a million pieces.

"I'd almost think that you liked me," I said hoarsely as I stared at the complicated, dangerous Alpha losing it...over me.

His body shuddered and then he turned around, so much emotion in his eyes that it took my already short breath almost completely away.

"You haven't realized that yet?" he said in a soft voice.

I would have answered him, but another coughing fit hit me and blood-splattered everything...and then I was out.

Pounding footsteps underneath me roused me from the darkness. I opened my eyes to see that we were outside. I was being carried in someone's arms as he took me towards the dock where I could see a speedboat approaching from a ways away. I turned my head and realized that it was Hendrix who had me. "Hold on, little wolf. River's almost here. He has the witch."

"Okay," I tried to say, but the word got stuck in my throat. Pinpricks of pain were beating at me all over my body, interspersed with numbness that actually scared me more than the pain. We got to the dock, but Hendrix didn't slow down until we'd gotten to the farthest point of it.

"River," Hendrix roared out to the sea as if he could somehow get the speedboat here faster. A wave beat against the side of the dock, and I felt the spray of the water fall on my face, the coolness feeling like heaven in the face of the pain.

"Stay with me, baby," came Caspian's voice from beside

us. I didn't have the strength to look at him, but I felt him grasp my ankle tightly, letting him know that I was there.

The sound of the speedboat grew to a roar as it came closer until the sound was almost deafening as it slowed to the dock.

Caspian rushed forward, and I glanced over to see him helping pull the speedboat in.

"She's fading fast," barked Hendrix.

"We would've gotten here sooner, but we ran into the Manchurians," explained River, his anger and frustration clear.

I had no idea who they were, and I didn't care as another attack of coughing up blood hit me.

I was staring listlessly at River who was standing next to a wizened old woman in the boat. I assumed she was the witch. At the sound of my coughing, he grabbed the woman and jumped out of the boat, much to the woman's shock and chagrin. On any other occasion, the look on her face would've been amusing. But not now.

The woman was not a shifter, her looks made that clear. But she was some kind of supernatural. Even from a few feet away, I could feel power emanating from her. And it was a hell of a lot of power, especially considering she was a tiny thing, only coming up to River's chest. She had black hair liberally streaked with gray and vibrant orange-looking eyes that reminded me of a cat's. It was a shade I'd never seen before, and I stared at them half in a daze.

"Get everyone out of here," she barked, and Hendrix shot a glare behind us and growled at the crowd that had gathered. I could hear footsteps rapidly moving away.

The woman pushed up her sleeves and gestured at me. "Are you just going to stand there? Or are you going to lay her down so I can actually look at her?"

Hendrix huffed at her tone but immediately stooped to the ground to lay me down gently. He stroked my cheek with the back of his hand, sadness and yearning in his gaze.

"You have my payment?" the witch asked, looking at Hendrix challengingly. She pointed her thumb at River. "He assured me you would have it."

"She didn't want the money I'd brought," River snapped in a surly, annoyed voice.

"What are you wanting then?" Hendrix asked. He paused for a moment and then continued. "Name your price." My eyes blinked up at him, my brain struggling to understand why he would offer something like that.

The witch's gaze grew greedy at the desperation heavy in the air, and she made a humming noise. "A drop of your blood will do," she said happily.

I heard River and Caspian try to stifle their gasps. An Alpha's blood was precious, imbued with power from the Moon Goddess herself. But add in the fact that there was something more to the three of them, powers I'd never heard existing in any other shifter, what she was asking for was a steep price.

I expected Hendrix to refuse, even after he told her to name her price. There was no telling what the witch would do with the drop of his blood.

"Very well," Hendrix said through gritted teeth, not even hesitating for a second.

"I want a drop of blood from all of you," she clarified, sensing the power she held at that moment.

Maybe I was going to die.

It was one thing for River to rush and get this woman on Hendrix's order, but for River to give up his essence in exchange for my life, for him to endanger himself...

"I agree," responded Caspian with no hesitation.

"I accept your price as well," echoed River. Looking around at everyone, the only person that seemed shocked by River's sacrifice was me.

I put that away to examine for later, if I survived.

"Heal her first, and then you'll get your payment," ordered Hendrix.

The witch laughed, sounding far younger than what her appearance would suggest. "I wasn't born yesterday, young pup. You'll give me at least a partial payment or nothing is going to happen."

Out of the corner of my eye, I saw Caspian reach for the gun around his waist, but River grabbed his arm before he could unholster it.

"You can have a drop of mine first," said Hendrix, and the witch grinned victoriously.

I really didn't like this woman.

She hustled over to him, her orange eyes beginning to glow as she pulled a small glass vial from her pocket.

Convenient.

The witch held the vial in one hand while she began to circle her other hand in the air above it, peering up at Hendrix greedily.

My gut swirled with dread as I watched them. I couldn't let him do this.

"Hendrix, don't," I whimpered out in a raspy voice. But it wasn't very effective since, at that moment, blood began to pour out of my nose. That was a new symptom. My whole body started to shake, and I began to froth from my mouth. My eyes rolled to the back of my head as my shaking intensified.

There was shouting, and then hands were on me, pushing me to the side. The shaking seemed to last forever, and by the time it finally stopped, I was ready to die.

"Do it," I heard Hendrix roar.

"This blood freely given, to use as I would choose," the witch began to chant over and over again.

I watched in shocked horror as an orange glow spread from the vial to the hand that Hendrix was not holding up.

Hendrix gritted his teeth like he was in pain, and a bead of sweat trailed down his face. His hand began to shake, and my eyes widened as I saw a single drop of blood pulled from his pointer finger, traveling through the orange glow until it dropped into the vial.

The witch stopped her chanting and quickly plugged the top of the vial, the orange glow disappearing.

Hendrix dropped his hand and clenched his fists before taking a step away from her.

"You got your payment. Now help her," he growled, and even an inch away from death, I could tell that he would have killed her right then under any other circumstance. The red glow in his eyes was rivaling the orange in hers.

Now we just need the rest of the rainbow, I crazily thought, since obviously, my brain wasn't working correctly.

The witch had the audacity to wink at him before striding over to me, and Hendrix's teeth began to extend before he turned around with a curse.

She sank to her knees beside me, much more agile than I would've expected for a woman of her age, pursing her lips as she looked me over.

"Our healer said her sickness was coming from those bands that prevent her shift."

"You chained your little pet, and now you want me to save her?" the witch said, sounding amused.

I hated her even more.

"We didn't put those on her, witch," River growled. "It was her old pack. They put it on her after-"

"After I was rejected," I finished for him in a gasp, wanting the witch to know the whole story...just in case she needed it.

"Times are indeed changing if a pretty little thing like you is getting rejected," she remarked callously.

The pain that I used to feel when reminded of my lost mate...wasn't there. Maybe it was the fact that I was dying...or maybe it was...them. The three complicated Alphas who'd kidnapped me.

The witch tapped on the band, and a shot of pain rushed through me. I moaned feebly, and the guys flinched like they wanted to jump to my aid.

"Easy, pups," she said distractedly, studying the bands closely. She murmured a few words in an unfamiliar language, and this time it wasn't just a shot of pain that I felt--it was a deluge of pain like I was being stabbed all over my body, a hundred times at once.

I was dehydrated, so there were no tears to cry. Instead, my body was just wracked with sobs, and my violent scream ripped through the air.

"Well, that didn't work," the witch muttered, sounding amused and showcasing what a raging psychopath she actually was.

"What the hell was that?" Caspian raged.

"It's not a precise process," she snapped back at him, sounding annoyed.

For the next half hour, she tried spell after spell...and none of them worked. And all of them were painful.

She stood up. "Where's my trunk?" she asked imperiously. "I need to look at the books I've brought."

"It's over there," snapped River, pointing at a worn trunk lying just outside the boat. He walked her over there as Hendrix and Caspian knelt down beside me.

"Just a little longer, little wolf," Hendrix murmured as he swept some of my sweaty hair out of my face.

"I have to tell you something."

My fingers twitched towards his hand, and he got the memo, moving his hand so it enveloped mine.

"Just in case I don't get the chance...I'm glad you rejected her. And I'm glad he rejected me. Because it meant you all got to be mine, for at least a moment," I whispered, the words so faint I wasn't even sure that he and Caspian could even hear them.

"You are mine—ours," Hendrix amended with a glance at Caspian. There was a glint of humor on Caspian's face, but it was quickly replaced by the worry and fear that had been present since I'd fallen ill. "I'm glad you've finally realized that."

I snorted, and another gush of blood rushed out, effectively ruining whatever moment I'd been creating.

There was another word on my tongue, one that threatened to burst out. I clamped down on my tongue, too prideful to say such a thing even in the face of the end.

And besides, that wasn't what this really was. Right?

My body started seizing again, and that was the end of that.

When I woke up, the witch was kneeling in front of me again, holding a book open with one hand as she murmured more strange words over the bands. I wondered how long I'd been out this time. Nothing seemed to have changed though. The bands were definitely still on, and I definitely still felt like I was dying.

"Ahah!" she finally shouted with glee, making me flinch. Then she pursed her lips as she flipped through a few pages.

"I haven't seen this level of dark magic before from a random pack," she said. "What pack did you say you were from?" she asked, seeming to be much more interested in me than she had this entire time.

"It doesn't matter, witch. Can you help her?"

Displeasure flickered across her face, but she took a deep breath and calmed her features. For a second, something shimmered beneath her skin, and I saw a flash of scales and sharp teeth that peeked through her wrinkles. But when I blinked...it was gone. It was hell not knowing whether something was real or if I was just imagining it because of whatever was wrong with me.

The witch silently flipped through a few pages before evidently finding whatever spell she was looking for. "How long did you say she'd been sick for?" she asked Hendrix.

"Six days," he responded.

"She only has hours left then," she responded calmly while the three Alphas all had silent freak-outs around us.

Me, I just felt resigned. If this wasn't dying, then I couldn't imagine what it was really like.

She pulled out a wicked-looking knife that looked like it had been carved from a bone, and Hendrix made a move to take it away from her. "I need this for the spell, you idiot," she hissed.

He nodded, a tic in his cheek showcasing how much he was hating life right now. She turned back towards me and suddenly sliced the inside of her hand, dripping blood all over the band around my wrists. The blood sizzled when it hit the bands, and smoke trailed off of them.

"Are you burning her?" Caspian asked worriedly, but he shut up as soon as River elbowed him.

Sweat began dripping down the witch's face as she murmured words so softly, I couldn't make them out. Her hands shook as she held them over the bands, and blood continued to stream from her hand all over my skin.

I watched in fear as her nose began bleeding and blood vessels in her eyes began to pop, but she didn't stop chanting.

Suddenly, there was a loud boom, and all the men were thrown backward at least twenty feet as if a bomb had gone off, only the witch and I weren't affected. I tried to move so I could make sure that the guys were alright from being thrown so far, but I found that I was unable to. It was like my entire body had become paralyzed. I couldn't even twitch my fingers. To add to my alarm, the witch's chanting began to falter as her whole body began to shake, not unlike what I'd been through multiple times since this had started.

Pressure built into the air, so thick and heavy that I would have screamed if I could open my mouth. The air pushed down around me, harder and harder until I was sure my skull was going to collapse and that would be it.

Just when I thought all hope was lost, it was as if a bubble popped around the witch and me, and all the pressure was suddenly gone. Fresh air was again brushing against my face.

My bands crumbled into dust at that moment, and black smoke filtered from my wrists. For a second, I could see what looked like a nightmarish face looking out from the smoke. It bared razor-sharp teeth, fury written all over its face.

The witch commanded something in that language I didn't understand, and the smoke dissipated with a wave of her hand until it was completely gone. She then toppled to her back, her breath coming out in gasps as she worked to recover from the spell she'd just done.

I was only faintly aware of her though, because I'd just realized...I was free.

The spell had worked. All the sickness I'd been feeling was gone, and there was a lightness inside of me that I hadn't felt since—since the bands had first been put on. It was more than just feeling free, though; it was feeling my wolf again like the Moon Goddess had always intended. She was so clear to me now, I could practically feel her fur brushing against me, sensing her eagerness to come out after being trapped for so long.

"Little wolf, are you okay?" Hendrix asked as he ran up to me as I struggled to get up. I could see Caspian and River sitting up as well in the same places they had been thrown. I was pretty sure they'd been knocked out.

I moved my body around, holding up my wrists and staring at them in amazement. I took a deep breath, delighted that my lungs didn't hurt when I breathed, I no longer felt nauseous, and as I looked into Hendrix's beautiful face…it didn't transform into any scary monsters.

I'd been cured.

My wolf barked inside of me, reminding me that she'd been waiting a long time to come out, and she didn't care how sexy Hendrix looked standing over us with locks of his hair falling in his face. She was ready to be free.

"I feel amazing," I told him, right before I closed my eyes and let my wolf take over.

Despite the fact that it had been years since I'd been able to shift, it might as well have been as easy as breathing.

One second I was me, and then the next second I was *her*. I watched through my wolf's eyes as Hendrix's gaze widened, shocked to see my wolf standing where I'd just been.

"Hello there, beautiful," he purred, and despite my wolf's earlier thoughts about being so excited to run, she was totally thinking about falling on her back and letting Hendrix rub her belly. She was fickle like that, apparently.

"You're a pretty girl, aren't you," said Caspian as he walked towards us. My wolf bounded towards him, jumping up on his chest and almost pushing him over as she licked all over his face, to his surprise and delight. My wolf wasn't just pretty; in my opinion, she was definitely as beautiful as Hendrix had first said. I'd obviously only seen my wolf once, but it was definitely something I wouldn't ever forget. She was a snowy white color all over except for the right front paw, which was an ebony color. The contrast was quite striking, and my wolf was very proud of her looks.

He cooed at us like we were small children, which my wolf loved, and he stroked our hair softly.

"Want to run, baby?" he asked, and my wolf yipped in

excitement, bouncing off of him and beginning to run in circles excitedly while kicking up sand. Abruptly, our feet slid out from under us and we rolled over to our back. I could hear the guys laughing softly, but my wolf wasn't embarrassed at all.

Suddenly, there was an enormous chocolate brown wolf beside me, and I knew immediately it was Caspian, his manly scent flooding me. He returned my earlier favor by licking me in the face and then taking off in a run down the beach, barking at me to follow after. When he was shifted, Caspian was whole, all four of his legs were there. He was a sight to behold.

My wolf was about to take off when suddenly I was tackled by a stunning blue-grey wolf that towered over me. This had to be River. The jerkwad. He stared down at me happily, his tongue hanging out of his mouth, and then he licked my wolf's snout softly, like he was kissing me.

My wolf melted immediately, totally in love, and I had to remind her sternly we weren't quite sure about River yet. Even if we had slept together.

She reluctantly agreed with me and abruptly licked the underside of River's snout before wriggling out from under him and setting off after Caspian's wolf. Looking backward, we could see Hendrix watching over us wistfully. I had never asked if his only form was the monstrous wolf I'd seen in the city. I could see how he would have to save his shifts for certain times if that was the case.

My wolf, being the softy she was, stopped suddenly, almost falling over as she switched directions and tore back to where Hendrix was standing. River barked at us as he ran along beside us, and my wolf kicked up sand in his face...just so he would know who was boss.

I ran until I was right in front of Hendrix and then

decided to just go for it, jumping up on his chest like I had with Caspian and licking his face.

Hendrix laughed, and my wolf shivered in delight at the sound. Something inside of me flickered, like starlight was bouncing around my insides.

Before my wolf did anything else, the witch chose that moment to get up off the ground. I probably would have felt guilty that the rest of us had been playing while she recovered from my life-saving spell...but she was a bitch. My opinion on that had not changed.

I was very grateful to the bitch, though.

She looked a mess. Blood was smeared around her nose, and her eyes were still bloodshot. I'm sure my human form looked far worse, though.

She smoothed her hair back and scowled at me. "I'm ready for my payment," she snapped. My stomach curdled with dread, all the joy leaking out of me as I was reminded of the price.

Hendrix whistled, and I turned to see Caspian bounding towards us, shifting to his human form mid-step when he was almost here. River had shifted as well, and I knew I probably should, but my wolf really didn't want to quite yet.

I'll let you out as soon as this is done, I told her before forcing the shift back, much to her disgruntlement.

The air grew somber as we gathered around, watching as she pulled another vial out to collect her payment.

"I'm sorry," I whispered softly to Caspian and River.

Caspian was suddenly in my face, holding my chin tightly as he forced me to look at him. "This is nothing compared to what I would do for you," he growled, all the lightheartedness that I was used to with him completely gone. His lips crashed down onto mine in a searing hot, all-consuming kiss that set my body on fire. His tongue pushed into my mouth, tangling gently, yet insistently with my tongue until I was a mindless, horny mess.

He pulled away, and I realized that he'd managed to replace all the guilt I'd been feeling with his special brand of warmth.

It was a funny thing, but I'd never felt like I was really worth anything in my life. Having your dad try and kill you, and then your mate reject you, did that to a girl.

But just maybe...

"I don't have all day," the witch sniffed angrily.

A low warning growl hitched from Hendrix's throat. He obviously didn't like her tone.

The witch gulped and managed to look a little bit chagrined...just a little bit though.

River thrust his hand out, and the witch quickly began her chant. Unlike the glow in Hendrix's extraction, a red glow built up between the vial and River's finger. River gritted his teeth, snarling in pain as the drop of blood was extracted and deposited in the jar. He quickly dropped his hand and stepped away, a quick shiver passing through his body.

The witch looked like she was about to have an orgasm as she put the topper in the vial and hid it away.

Then it was Caspian's turn. He looked a bit green at the prospect, but he shot me a wink and stepped up to take his turn. Caspian bit his lip as a yellow glow stretched between his finger and the vial. A trail of blood streamed from how hard he was biting. The blood from his lip wasn't good enough apparently, because she did her chant until a drop had been taken from his finger and deposited in the vial.

And then it was done.

"Fuck," Caspian muttered before taking a few steps away and throwing up.

"I'll escort you back," said River, obviously eager for her to be away from the compound.

The witch looked like she was about to do a jig, she seemed so happy. There was no sign of the strain from the spell she'd conducted on me. She was practically glowing now. The unease only grew as River escorted her with seven other guards towards the boat.

"Thank you," I called after her, needing to at least acknowledge that she'd both saved and changed my life today.

The witch didn't even bother to look back.

"What will she be able to do with your blood?" I asked.

"Everything will be fine, little wolf," Hendrix answered, deliberately not answering my question. "Now, how about another run so I can see your pretty wolf again?"

Caspian had recovered by now from throwing up, and he grinned before shifting into his stunning wolf.

I followed him into my shift, my wolf once again taking control. We spent the rest of the evening playing around on the beach, with Hendrix watching over us.

It was amazing the difference between how I'd woken up and how the day had ended.

When I finally passed out that night, Caspian wrapped around me, I was so tired that I didn't even dream.

Chapter 12

Syn

"I have a surprise for you," Caspian purred as he appeared in my doorway a week after I'd been cured. He was dressed in a simple, white linen shirt and a pair of loose tan pants. But I had the urge to eat him. All that tan, golden skin was a temptation that was hard to ignore.

"You can lick me later, ladybug," Caspian said with a cocky smirk. "First, you have to look at this." He pulled a thick envelope from behind his back and strode towards me, tossing it in my lap after giving me a hot, licking kiss that had me leaning forward, desperate for more.

He laughed and stepped out of my reach. "You're going to want to see what's in this."

I rolled my eyes and huffed before picking up the thick, cream envelope. My name in fancy, glittering cursive caught my eye, and I frowned before carefully opening it up.

The words *Shifter Falls University* were the first thing to catch my eye, and I stared at it in disbelief, not understanding what I was seeing even as I pulled the first letter out and began to read.

"I am delighted to inform you that you have been admitted

to attend Shifter Falls University..." the letter began. I read the entire thing, a strange tingling sensation floating over me as I did so.

"I don't understand," I whispered as I traced my name on the letter.

I looked up at him, tears burning in my eyes. "Is this some kind of joke?" I growled, throwing the paper away from me.

"What? No!" Caspian said in a panicked voice, looking confused.

"I never went to school past sixth grade, Caspian. How the fuck did I all of a sudden get admission to the top shifter school in the country? Why would you do this?"

"I'm not sure what's happening here," said Caspian, holding up his hands beseechingly. "We thought you would be happy about this!"

A hitched sob came out of my mouth. I knew I was overreacting, but it was like my mind couldn't comprehend this. Not being allowed to go to school had been one of the worst things to ever happen to me in a long list of bad things. I hadn't ever dreamed of going to college, let alone a school like Shifter Falls.

"Little wolf, I wouldn't have given up a drop of my very fucking essence to an insane witch just to turn around and hurt you," growled Hendrix, stalking in from the doorway where he'd evidently been listening. "Haven't we proven to you yet that nothing is impossible when it comes to us? If you tell us you want the fucking moon, I'm pretty sure I could figure out a way to get it for you."

"So, you're letting me leave?" I asked breathlessly, my mind suddenly filled with farfetched images of walking around a campus draped with colorful autumn leaves, tall, red-bricked colonial buildings surrounding me.

"Let you leave?" Hendrix asked in a cold, dangerous voice,

bringing my attention back to him. My shoulders dipped back, realizing I'd done something wrong.

"Caspian, how about you leave us for now."

"I think this can all be smoothed over," said Caspian warily, eyeing Hendrix like he was about to attack, which maybe he was.

"Leave!" Hendrix growled, and Caspian's hands extended into claws as he fought against Hendrix's command. Finally, his jaw went up and he bared his throat before leaving the room.

Hendrix, Caspian, and River were all Alphas, but even with all of their dominance, there was no denying that Hendrix was always the apex predator in the room.

And right now, I was alone with the predator.

"I thought I made it clear that you would never be leaving me," he said silkily, one of his fingertips extending into his terrifying monster claws. He trailed the tip of the nail across my throat and then down my arm, sending shivers coursing down my body.

My wolf had already flopped over inside of me, baring her belly, and I was about ready to join her.

"I'm confused then. How am I going to attend this college if I'm not allowed to leave? You going to come and be my personal professor?" I asked breathlessly as his claw sliced across my spaghetti strap.

"They offer their full courses online. You'll be able to take all the courses needed for graduation, and I'll have a tutor available to you every day to help you get through everything," he explained as his claw sliced through my other strap, and I barely caught it before it bared my braless chest.

Even with the fear flickering across my skin, I couldn't help the wave of disappointment that hit me. For the one second that I'd imagined attending college, I'd imagined doing it free.

"You still want to get away. Even after everything that's happened, you're still thinking about getting away," he hissed, his claw-tipped hand gripping my chin, the sharp points puncturing my skin. "Did you think that I'd changed my mind somewhere along the way? When I said you belonged to me, what part of that did you not understand?"

My breath hitched, a weird mix of fear and lust barreling through me. I couldn't yank my face away. His claws would tear down my face. I still couldn't prevent the truth from snapping out. "You think that this can ever be real while I'm your prisoner? I've traded one cage for another, and this one may be gilded, but it's still just a cage, Hendrix. How long can this really last when I'm nothing but a possession?"

A silence had never felt so loud as our eyes stayed locked, clashing against each other.

His hand suddenly moved from my face to around my throat, gripping it tight enough that I could only breathe in gasps.

"Let's get one thing straight, little wolf. You are my possession. You are my obsession. You are my fucking everything."

"Am I your love?" I whispered. I wished I had cut my fucking tongue out of my mouth as soon as the words slipped out.

He answered with a growl, and his grip tightened until the edges of my vision started to fade into black.

"A man like me isn't capable of love, little wolf. You'll only be disappointed if you go looking for that."

He finally loosened his grip enough to let me breathe. I closed my eyes, breaking our stare-off. A tear slid down my cheek, and he abruptly licked it off.

"You should have no problem letting me go, then," I whispered.

"Never," he snarled before his lips crashed against mine.

He pushed me back onto the bed. My legs parted against

my will as he slipped between them. Hendrix pressed down against me, grinding against my clit as he moved and stoking feelings that I was desperate not to have. His hands fisted in my hair, tugging my head where he wanted it as he devoured my mouth from every possible angle. I tried to push him away, but he might as well have been an impenetrable stone for as much headway as I made.

His chest was all muscles under my touch, and smooth skin that in any other circumstance I would have been salivating over, but not right now. Right now, I hated him for reminding me that no matter how good life here may seem, I'd always just be a prisoner.

I clawed at his back, and he hissed at the sting of pain and restrained my arms. Unable to move, I sunk my teeth into the flesh right above his nipple. Hendrix cursed, and my arms slipped from his grasp. I immediately started pushing at his chest again to get him away.

Was it really going to be like this? Was this really happening after everything?

One of his hands fisted my hair, holding my head arched back. It was just on the edge of painful, and I glared at him, tears running down my face. Hendrix gazed at me, his expression full of anger, that red gleam of his shining from his eyes that told me his wolf was firmly in control.

My breath was coming out in gasps, and I could feel my heartbeat soaring out of control in my chest. I'd never felt more like I was in the grasp of a predator than I did at this moment. With his clawed hand, he savagely ripped at my clothes until I was lying naked beneath him. I shivered in fear as I stared up at him.

He lowered his head abruptly and pressed his lips against mine. I was expecting his kiss to be savage, but his lips were soft as they moved, even as he trapped me against the bed. My traitorous body melted at his kiss. He took his time, kissing me slowly, sipping at my mouth like I was a glass of fine champagne.

Even when his hand released its grip on my hair, I didn't find the will in me to move my traitorous body. All of a sudden, I was wrapping my arms around him, holding onto him instead of pushing him away. What was wrong with me?

He moved away from my lips, and I just stared at him, faintly aware of the tears still streaking down my face. They didn't seem to affect him though. He began to move down my face, licking away the tears, nibbling at my neck, his tongue arcing down my body in decadent, sensual swirls that had my core throbbing. He was soft across my breasts, lightly biting down on my nipple and making me moan.

"I hate you," I whispered even as his head dipped lower.

He didn't seem to care, because his breath was hot across my skin as his hand trailed down to sweep across my clit, sending shockwaves across my skin. His finger moved in between my folds, and I hated myself along with him at that moment, because I knew I was soaking wet.

"That's my good little wolf," he purred, as his fingers expertly danced across my clit.

I briefly came back to life when his head moved in between my legs, and I tried to close them to keep him out. He pushed my legs apart like I wasn't even trying, and then he began to lick and suck on my clit until I was a writhing, panting mess. I hated the pleasure coursing through my body. I hated that he had this much control over me, that he knew exactly how to play my body like an expert violinist.

My body felt like it was going to burn up as he continued to suck on me, adding his fingers once more to the mix. They pushed inside of me, moving in time with his tongue. I could feel my orgasm building up inside of me, and as much as I didn't want it, there was nothing I could do to stop it.

He was too skilled. My body loved it too much.

I fell over the cliff with a loud moan, my entire body trembling as the pleasure shot through me.

It was a strange thing, to feel so good and detest something so much.

He finally pulled his head out from between my legs, and I snapped them close. He was wearing a triumphant grin, his lips shiny with my release.

And I hated him. I hated him so fucking much.

I turned my head away, determined that if he was going to take the next step, then at least I could look away, try to imagine I was anywhere else but there.

He leaned over me, and I braced my body for his next touch. "I'll always own you, little wolf," he whispered sensually in my ear as his finger took one more swipe across my aching, sopping wet folds. Out of the corner of my eye, I saw him lick his fingers clean of me, and then he moved away and leisurely strode out of the room...leaving me ruined.

It took a minute for the tears to start, but once they did, they didn't stop. Not for hours and hours.

The tears finally dried up around three a.m. I sat by my window, listening to the sounds of the waves in the distance crashing against the beach. As I sat there, I suddenly saw a familiar figure meandering clumsily from the mansion, out across the courtyard lights, and through the gate.

It was River.

I don't know why I did it, but I went after him.

Hendrix hadn't bothered to lock my door after what happened; at this point, he was confident in the fact that he owned me...as he displayed earlier tonight. The whole mansion was eerily quiet, though, as I slipped through the halls; I didn't come across one guard my entire walk.

I made it out into the courtyard, breathing in the salty air like it could somehow cleanse me of the night's events. I made my way out into the streets, feeling uneasy now because I was still not seeing guards.

But with the way River was walking, he could have been sleepwalking. And even though I shouldn't care, I didn't want him to get hurt.

Plus, maybe I could talk to him about what happened with Hendrix, gain an ally or something.

I got to the beach and found him stumbling along the water's edge.

"River!" I called out, just as a giant wave, chose that moment to take him out.

I sprinted towards the water, continuing to scream his name. The lighting from the walls was dim, and I couldn't make out anything in the inky blackness of the water. Suddenly, I saw him crawling out from the water, gasping and coughing as he did so.

I ran towards him and helped him get farther from the waves that were threatening to take us both back out there.

"Syn?" he asked breathlessly. "I was asleep. I almost drowned myself," he sputtered, wrapping his arms around me and soaking my nightgown as he held on to me for dear life.

"I saw you out the window and decided to come after you," I explained, my heart still racing from what just happened.

"How did no one stop me?" River asked after a minute, pulling away from me minutely and searching around like he expected a guard to appear at any minute.

But the strange thing was, I couldn't even see the outlines of guards up in the towers on the wall. There should have been lights up there, but they were perfectly dark.

River stumbled to his feet. "Something's not right," he

murmured, holding me close to him as he scanned our surroundings. "We need to get—"

Before he could finish his sentence, the sound of a gun being cocked came from behind us.

Gleaming sharp teeth were all that I saw before there was a faint rush of air, and then something stabbed me right in the throat. My hand reached to grab it as I gasped, and my fingertips touched something that felt like glass.

I heard River grunt in pain next to me, but there was nothing I could do...

A second later, everything went black.

Find out the conclusion to Syn's story HERE!

I didn't mean to take the wrong road.

I didn't mean to make it to that small town.

And I didn't mean to meet two men, who set me and my wolf on fire.

But here I am somehow, and peace is the last thing I've found.

And don't forget about the serial killer...

Get your copy of Wild Moon today!

Chapter 1

RUNE

I was cursed.

That had to be it.

I'd come to this conclusion somewhere on the highway, lost in the middle of nowhere, in a strip of land so empty and so flat, it made you feel like you were the only person on the planet. Hours after my car had been broken into while I used the restroom, leaving me with only a twenty-dollar bill to my name.

I'd been driving for weeks...or was it months already? And the only conclusion for why my life had thus far been a giant shit show of the most epic proportions was because I was cursed.

I was perhaps also an idiot.

The sun was falling in the west, and the sky was a kaleidoscope of color. A mixture of pinks and reds that at one point, would have made me shed a tear, back when I had a heart that could still be affected by beautiful things.

Alistair had sucked all the beauty out of my life, twisted and tore at my heart until it was incapable of viewing the world as it once had.

And yet something inside of me, something that was irrevocably tied to him for forever, it still missed him. Despite what he had done, what he'd kept from me. Despite the fact that I'd been told my whole life how wonderful my life was going to be once I found my true mate, and then he promptly destroyed any notions of happily ever after I'd ever dreamed about.

Despite all of that, I still wanted him.

And I always would. Because that's how true mates worked. It was a bond that forced you to need something, even if it would kill you.

Hence why I was thinking that I was cursed.

I dragged myself away from my pity party as the sun finally sank below the horizon. The landscape was changing around me. Jagged rocks were springing up from the land that I'd sworn had been flat as a board just a few minutes ago. Had I been lost in my head for that long? That wouldn't have been a surprise since I'd spent most of the last few weeks stuck in my head. I really needed to pay attention every once in a while though.

The landscape was definitely getting higher and higher, and I could see even steeper peaks up ahead. The road in front of me winded up through them. And now the sun was officially gone, and the stars were peaking their way out in the velvet sky.

Did I mention I was terrified of heights? And not just heights, add in driving and the dark too, and you officially had the trifecta of ridiculous fears that I'd developed over the years.

For a moment, I contemplated pulling over to the side of the road and trying to sleep until the morning. I quickly shook that thought away.

Despite the fact that a part of me wanted to be with Alistair, my true mate, desperately, all the other parts wanted to make sure we never saw that asshole again. The large majority of my parts also wanted to live, and Alistair would kill me after what I'd done. I knew that for a fact.

Taking a deep breath, I continued to drive, and it just kept getting darker and darker.

There were no lights out here, of course there wasn't. Because why put lights in the middle of nowhere? I put my brights on, not giving a fuck. If I was going to drive through a mountain range in the pitch black, you better believe I was going to be able to see while doing it.

Looking in my rearview mirror, I began to freak when I saw headlights approaching. Any time I saw another car, I wondered if it was Alistair, if somehow, he'd found me despite the crazy precautions I'd taken to be hidden from him. Like the way I'd snuck a stash of cash from Alistair's safe and bought a car with it when I was supposed to be grocery shopping. The way I'd used more of that cash to pay for everything I'd done on this road trip from hell. The way I'd gotten rid of my cell phone when I left so there was no way he could track it. The way I'd been wearing an ebony wig twenty-four-seven to try and change my looks.

I breathed a bit easier when I saw it was a Honda Accord. Alistair wouldn't be caught dead in a car that didn't scream money and privilege. While I was all about the practicality and the gas mileage of a Honda, Alistair wouldn't get in one no matter the circumstances, even if it was the only way to catch me.

My breathing increased however as the terrain began to rapidly ascend and I realized I was no longer approaching the mountain, I was going up the motherfucker.

There was a guardrail off to my right, but that didn't calm me down. I was now hyperventilating as I white-knuckled the steering wheel and leaned forward, trying to make sure I stayed right on that white line. If I was on that white line, then I wouldn't go off the edge. Right?

A loud honk had me jumping in my seat, swearing, and swerving the car. I hadn't handled unexpected things with grace over the last few years...but could I really be blamed for that after all that had happened?

I tore my eyes off the white line and glanced in the rearview, only to see that there were now a few cars lined up behind me. The driver behind me seemed to be waving his hands around.

Whoops. A glance at my speedometer showed that I was going about ten miles per hour right now. I highly doubted that was the speed limit, based on the cacophony of angry honks I was beginning to hear.

I rolled down my window, continuing to keep my eyes on that white line since my brain was filled with images of my car tumbling down the side of the mountain and bursting into flames fit for an action movie. I began to wave my arm out the window, trying to get them to go around me. Was there etiquette for this? Besides the obvious move of not driving forty miles under the speed limit.

The car behind me finally got the hint, and it swerved around me, honking loudly and rudely as it did so.

"Jerk," I muttered. The rest of the cars followed their leader, their brittle horns filling the night.

And then finally, it was just me.

Which maybe I hadn't been thinking through, because now that there weren't any other angry drivers to worry about, I was more aware than ever that I was painfully alone.

"What will it be like, Mama? When I find him," I whispered to my mother as she curled up beside me on the bed, a copy of Harry Potter *laying in her lap just as it was every night.*

"He'll make all your dreams come true, baby," she said with a gentle smile. "He'll see all the parts in your heart, and he'll accept them no matter what he finds."

"Why are there different parts in my heart?" I asked, the six-year-old me very confused about the words my mother was saying.

She giggled in that magical way of hers, and I watched entranced at the love I could see in her eyes. Was every mother that wonderful?

"I just mean, sweetheart, when you find him, you'll feel complete," she said sweetly as she brushed a piece of hair out of my eyes.

"Did you feel complete when you met Daddy?" I asked, sadness creeping down my throat at the blurry memory of a man as big as a bear who always smelled like peppermint and those cigarettes he used to smoke constantly as he anxiously paced around the room.

Something in my mother's eyes flickered and changed. There was a look there that I didn't recognize, but which made my little heart uncomfortable because it was so unfamiliar from the gentle looks my mother always gave me.

"Do you promise it will be like that?" I spit out, suddenly desperate for that look in her eyes to go away and for her to give me the reassurance I could always expect from her.

"I promise," she whispered, that look in her gaze fading slowly away.

I settled back into my pillows, ready to hear what Harry, Ron, and Hermoine were up to next, confident that the future was bright because my mother had said so.

Too bad my mother turned out to be a liar.

"Holy shit," I screeched, swerving out of the lane as something black…and furry, sprinted across the dim light of my headlights, startling me out of my journey to the past where I had no business spending time in the middle of the night in the freaking mountains.

"What the hell was that?" I whispered as I slowed down even more and tried to look around.

An even larger furry beast suddenly sprinted in front of my car, and this time, I yanked the steering wheel way too far to try not to hit it.

I screamed as my car went flying past that white line and careened off the embankment, the guardrails nowhere to be found. I went a few feet as I frantically pressed on the brake, those visions of my car tumbling down the mountains suddenly coming true right before my very eyes.

Was this how it ended? A sucktastic life ending with a fall down a mountain in the middle of nowhere.

Only me.

Shrubs and small trees...combined with my braking power, succeeded in slowing down my car, but the pine tree on the edge of the thick forest in front of me succeeded in stopping me completely. I choked on a scream as I hit the tree. The impact sending me flying forward as the airbags burst out of the steering wheel and door. I hadn't hit the tree very fast, but the force of the airbags sent me backwards, my neck whiplashing as it snapped back. The airbags ripped at my skin, burning my forearms, and a noxious plume of gas filled the air.

The silence after the crash was deafening for a long moment. But then a loud buzzing filled my ears as the adrenaline crashed against my veins. I coughed, wearily trying to wave my hand around to clear the air, the enormity of what had happened settling over my skin.

"Fuck," I gasped out. The human mind was truly exceptional. I mean, the fact that it could feel a myriad of emotions all at once as I was now.

Incredible.

"No, no, no," I cried out as I hit at the airbag and steering wheel in front of me.

My head and neck were beginning to hurt the longer I sat there, and a glance at my arms showed me that I did indeed have burns and lacerations from the stupid, fucking airbags.

"Okay, you can figure this out," I coached myself as I quit beating at my steering wheel and turned my attention to unlocking my seatbelt, which judging by the pain I felt in my chest, had definitely stopped me from flying through the windshield.

Small mercies.

After the seatbelt was successfully dismantled, I struggled against the car door, the movement sending agony against my protesting muscles. *This is why you shouldn't live on gas station snacks and fast food for weeks on end*, I thought to myself. *Maybe it wouldn't be so hard to open a small thing like a car door if my muscles actually existed in my arms anymore.*

Success! The car door finally flew open, and I promptly fell out of my seat into the shrubs and rocks that were waiting for me just outside. Apparently, my legs weren't working anymore.

I shivered as I looked around. Somehow, my lights were still working, and the area around me was eerily illuminated.

There was a thick forest just ahead of me. And although I couldn't see anything...it felt like something was watching me.

I shivered again and decided it was best to try and get to the road and see if I could flag someone down for help. Although really, that was probably worse than staying here by the trees. I'd seen the news, I knew the danger of trying to hitchhike, especially out in the middle of nowhere like this. With my luck, I'd get picked up by a mugger or a murderer...or even Alistair. And not to mention those two animals I'd seen...

I groaned and reached back into the car to grab the tiny flashlight from my door that I'd picked up at...you guessed it...a gas station, and then I limped my way back towards the road, which was a seriously difficult task since I'd fallen down a shallow embankment. The roots, rocks, and weeds didn't exactly help. I was not a hiker. I was only a few feet away from the road when a howl ripped through the air. I stopped in my tracks. That thing inside of me that had been there for as long as I could remember perked up at the sound. There was a time that a wolf's howl meant home. A time that I believed my howl would once call out into the night. My mother had promised that it would be a moment I would remember forever.

That was just another one of her lies.

Although I'd once welcomed the howl of a wolf, right now, the sound was a reminder that I was in the wilderness and there was a real possibility that I could be eaten. There weren't any shifters out here, I'd seen the map many times as Alistair tried to plan world domination or whatever it was that he was interested in. Which meant the howl I was hearing was not a good sign.

Fuck, I sighed. I really was cursed. Deciding to proceed with my plan, I finally made it to the roadway, praying the next car that came by didn't contain a psychopath. I'd definitely already had my fair share of those.

I waited.

And I waited.

And I waited some more.

How was it I couldn't get cars off my ass earlier, and here I was, actually wanting cars to be on my ass, and they were nowhere to be seen? Had I taken a wrong turn somehow and stumbled upon a road that no one went down? I squinted at the road, trying to see if it looked like it was in disrepair. I hadn't noticed any out of the ordinary bumps.

"Are you fucking kidding me right now?" I screamed at the night sky, cursing at it for what felt like the millionth time.

Sighing and deciding I was going to just have to walk off this mountain myself, I set off down the dark road.

Weren't the stars supposed to be brighter out here? Where was the freaking moon?

I stumbled over a rock and barely caught myself with my hands. Of course, catching myself meant scraping my palms on the coarse asphalt and dropping my flashlight.

"Shit," I whispered, picking myself up and cradling my hands against me as the pain shot through me.

And there was a wolf howl again.

Perfect.

I'm sure the smell of my bloody palms was going to get me eaten alive.

Wouldn't that just be the most ironic way to go...ever.

I snorted, hysterical laughter threatening to spew from my mouth. I was definitely losing my mind.

Something shifted across the road just then, and I froze, the threat of laughter abruptly coming to a screeching halt.

I picked up my flashlight and began to jog down the road, despite the fact that I knew you were never supposed to run from a predator.

Where were all the fucking cars?

When nothing attacked me from behind, my confidence grew and I started to run faster, despite the fact that my legs were screaming in protest.

I came to a halt when a road that diverted from the main one I'd been running on appeared in front of me just a ways off. I hesitated and tried to squint farther down the main road. I should just stay on this road, right?

The sound of something running down the main road seemingly straight towards me made the decision for me, and I darted down the roadway and quickly realized that it was going downhill rather than uphill as the highway had headed. That was a good sign I thought.

I sighed again as I slowed down to a quick walk, the effects of the crash and my extremely poor diet over the last few weeks doing me in. If I had to run again because something was after me, I was probably going to have to accept it.

Damn those Cool Ranch Doritos.

The air was freezing here. I had on a stained *I Love New Mexico* shirt I'd found in one of my convenience store runs. It was pink, so I knew I had to have it. Alistair had hated pink, banned it from my wardrobe in fact...

Was it going to last forever, this way that my heart would squeeze every time I thought of him? How was it possible to hate someone with every fiber of your being but still feel like you couldn't breathe without them?

I stifled a sob, determined not to cry for him.

"Never again," I whispered to myself, even as his face appeared in my mind as I remembered the way he'd been looking at me right before he ripped my world into a million pieces that had no hope of ever being put back together.

I was so lost in my four hundred and twentieth pity party that it took me a while to notice the lights beginning to pop up in the distance and the enormous wooden sign with the symbol of what looked like a wolf carved above a scrawled 'Welcome to Amarok.'

Amarok? What kind of name was that? And why hadn't I seen this on the map I'd poured over before setting off today?

I pushed myself to go faster, the lights giving me hope, even if I was wary of getting so close to civilization. The places I'd picked had been out in the middle of nowhere. Small inns and motels where drifters and vagabonds passed through, perfect for a girl on the run. Alistair was a big fan of the Four Seasons, so the places I'd picked were, again, perfect for avoiding detection.

Another howl sounded through the night, and I decided that going near people, and hopefully getting help for my car, was a much better outcome than the possibility of getting eaten alive.

I already knew what a wolf's bite felt like, and it wasn't an experience I wanted to repeat...

Get your copy of Wild Moon today!

AUTHOR'S NOTE

Syn and her alphas are so delicious, are they not? We loved the idea of having a heroine who wasn't completely perfect, along with some of her men! We love this duet and hope you are loving it too! And that your Kindles are still working after that little cliffy.

But seriously...do you expect anything less at this point?

A huge thank you to Jasmine Jordan for coming in clutch with edits.

Another thank you to Summer, who stays up all night with us beta reading. Love you girl! You're such an amazing friend!

Thanks to Caitlin, our right hand woman, and the best friend and support system that you could ask for.

Thank you to our readers. We love you so much. You allow us to live our dreams. Thank you from the bottom of our hearts.

Until next time...

BOOKS BY C.R. JANE

www.crjanebooks.com

The Fated Wings Series

First Impressions

Forgotten Specters

The Fallen One (a Fated Wings Novella)

Forbidden Queens

Frightful Beginnings (a Fated Wings Short Story)

Faded Realms

Faithless Dreams

Fabled Kingdoms

Fated Wings 8

The Rock God (a Fated Wings Novella)

The Darkest Curse Series

Forget Me

Lost Passions

The Sounds of Us Contemporary Series (complete series)

Remember Us This Way

Remember You This Way

Remember Me This Way

<u>Broken Hearts Academy Series: A Bully Romance (complete duet)</u>

Heartbreak Prince

<u>Heartbreak Lover</u>

<u>Ruining Dahlia (Contemporary Mafia Standalone)</u>

<u>Ruining Dahlia</u>

<u>Hades Redemption Series</u>

The Darkest Lover

The Darkest Kingdom

<u>Monster & Me Duet Co-write with Mila Young</u>

Monster's Plaything

<u>Academy of Souls Co-write with Mila Young (complete series)</u>

School of Broken Souls

School of Broken Hearts

School of Broken Dreams

School of Broken Wings

<u>Fallen World Series Co-write with Mila Young (complete series)</u>

Bound

Broken

Betrayed

<u>Belong</u>

<u>Thief of Hearts Co-write with Mila Young (complete series)</u>

Siren Condemned

Siren Sacrificed

Siren Awakened

Siren Redeemed

Kingdom of Wolves Co-write with Mila Young

Wild Moon

Wild Heart

Wild Girl

Wild Love

Wild Soul

Stupid Boys Series Co-write with Rebecca Royce

Stupid Boys

Dumb Girl

Crazy Love

Breathe Me Duet Co-write with Ivy Fox (complete)

Breathe Me

Breathe You

Rich Demons of Darkwood Series Co-write with May Dawson

Make Me Lie

Make Me Beg

Books By Mila Young

www.milayoungbooks.com

Shadowlands

Shadowlands Sector, One

Shadowlands Sector, Two

Shadowlands Sector, Three

Shadows & Wolves Complete Collection

Chosen Vampire Slayer

Night Kissed

Moon Kissed

Blood Kissed

The Alpha-Hole Duet

Real Alphas Bite

Kingdom of Wolves

Wild Moon

Wild Heart

Wild Girl

Wild Love

Winter's Thorn

To Seduce A Fae

To Tame A Fae

Cursed (Beauty and the Beast Retelling)

Entangled (Rapunzel Retelling)

Princess of Frost (Snow Queen)

Thief of Hearts Series Co-write with C.R. Jane

Siren Condemned

Siren Sacrificed

Siren Awakened

Broken Souls Series Co-write with C.R. Jane

School of Broken Souls

School of Broken Hearts

School of Broken Dreams

School of Broken Wings

Fallen World Series Co-write with C.R. Jane

Bound

Broken

Betrayed

Belong

Beautiful Beasts Academy

Manicures and Mayhem

Diamonds and Demons

Hexes and Hounds

Secrets and Shadows

Passions and Protectors

Ancients and Anarchy

Subscribe to Mila Young's Newsletter to receive exclusive content, latest updates, and giveaways. Join here.

About C.R. Jane

A Texas girl living in Utah now, I'm a wife, mother, lawyer, and now author. My stories have been floating around in my head for years, and it has been a relief to finally get them down on paper. I'm a huge Dallas Cowboys fan and I primarily listen to Beyonce and Taylor Swift...don't lie and say you don't too.

My love of reading started probably when I was three and with a faster than normal ability to read, I've devoured hundreds of thousands of books in my life. It only made sense that I would start to create my own worlds since I was always getting lost in others'.

I like heroines who have to grow in order to become badasses, happy endings, and swoon-worthy, devoted, (and hot) male characters. If this sounds like you, I'm pretty sure we'll be friends.

I'm so glad to have you on my team...check out the links below for ways to hang out with me and more of my books you can read!

Visit my **Facebook** page to get updates.

Visit my **Amazon Author** page.

Visit my Website.

Sign up for my newsletter to stay updated on new releases, find out random facts about me, and get access to different points of view from my characters.

About Mila Young

Best-selling author, Mila Young tackles everything with the zeal and bravado of the fairytale heroes she grew up reading about. She slays monsters, real and imaginary, like there's no tomorrow. By day she rocks a keyboard as a marketing extraordinaire. At night she battles with her mighty pen-sword, creating fairytale retellings, and sexy ever after tales. In her spare time, she loves pretending she's a mighty warrior, walks on the beach with her dogs, cuddling up with her cats, and devouring every fantasy tale she can get her pinkies on.

Ready to read more and more from Mila Young? Subscribe today here.

Join Mila's **Wicked Readers group** for exclusive content, latest news, and giveaway. Click here.

For more information...
milayoungauthor@gmail.com

www.ingramcontent.com/pod-product-compliance
Lightning Source LLC
Chambersburg PA
CBHW071147180726

48291CB00007B/2356